AUTHORS OF OUR

DANIELLE ACKLEY-MCPHAIL

BETH CATO

JAMES CHAMBERS

EF DEAL

CHRISTINE NORRIS

CYNTHIA RADTHORNE

AARON ROSENBERG

HILDY SILVERMAN

DAVID LEE SUMMERS

JEFF YOUNG

STEAMPUNK TITLES BY ESPEC BOOKS

THE CLOCKWORK CHRONICLES
The Clockwork Witch
The Clockwork Solution
The Clockwork Discovery (Forthcoming)
(MICHELLE D. SONNIER)

Baba Ali and the Clockwork Djinn
(DANIELLE ACKLEY-MCPHAIL AND DAY AL-MOHAMED)

A Curse of Ash and Iron
A Curse of Time and Memory (Forthcoming)
(CHRISTINE NORRIS)

Spirit Seeker
(JEFF YOUNG)

Sherman's Last Round-Up
(DAVID SHERMAN)

Esprit De Corpse
Aeros & Heroes (Forthcoming)
(EF DEAL)

Crimson Whisper
(KEN SCHRADER)

STEAMPUNK ANTHOLOGIES BY ESPEC BOOKS

FORGOTTEN LORE
A Cast of Crows
A Cry of Hounds

After Punk:
Steampowered Tales of the Afterlife

Gaslight & Grimm
Grimm Machinations

Grease Monkeys:
The Heart and Soul of Dieselpunk

The Weird Wild West

The Chaos Clock: Tales of Cosmic Aether

OTHER AETHER

Tales of Global Steampunk

edited by

GREG SCHAUER AND
DANIELLE ACKLEY-MCPHAIL

eBooks

Pennsville, NJ

PUBLISHED BY
eSpec Books LLC
Danielle McPhail,
Publisher
PO Box 242,
Pennsville, New Jersey 08070
www.especbooks.com

ISBN: 978-1-956463-33-0
ISBN (ebook): 978-1-956463-32-3

"On the Wings of an Angel" originally published in *In An Iron Cage* by Dark Quest Books, 2011.

Cover and Interior Design: Danielle McPhail, McP Digital Graphics

Illustrations:
Art Credits - www.Shutterstock.com
Cover:
Airships over old mine © Melkor3D
A large vintage, ancient world map, drawn by hand with dragons, sea monsters and ancient sailboats. Adventures and pirates, ancient treasures and quests © Harbar Liudmyla

Interior:
Vintage dividers and borders © Seamartini Graphics, www.fotolia.com

FOR THOSE WHO THIRST
TO EXPLORE THE WIDER WORLD.

Contents

The Kami of the Mountain

Cynthia Radthorne

RIPPLES OF MOONLIGHT.

That's what it looked like to Miako as she gazed out across the flooded rice paddy. The night sky loomed above her, the moon gathering the stars around like family.

She knew the ripples in the paddy were not really light, just the water reflecting the sky. And yet... The god of the moon, Tsukiyomi, created that light and gave it to the earth. Did that not make what the water gave to her part of that same celestial offering? Moonlight down from the sky, here at her feet...

She shook her head with a little laugh, her silken hair catching some of that same lunar light as she did so. *I am being silly*, she told herself. *I am out here for a purpose, not to be musing over gods and moons.*

Opening her canvas bag, she pulled out the latest version of her little invention, a metal box with eight spindly legs like some sort of clockwork spider. Setting it down carefully in an as-yet unplanted section of the rice field, the box just above the surface of the shallow water, she made sure the articulated legs were all oriented in the correct direction. Retrieving a small pouch from her bag, she filled the tiny hopper atop her spider-box with rice seeds.

Satisfied, she took hold of the large wind-up key at the back of the box and gave it three solid twists all the way around. With a gentle whirring, one little leg rose up and extended forward, then another did the same. As both legs contracted, the next pair started the same movements until all the legs began a similar dance in sequence, propelling the spider-box forward.

Miako saw the gear-driven little scooper extend below the box into the water, knowing it would make a nice hole in the soil below. A quiet little *snick* told her the hopper had opened, dropping a few seeds through the sieve at the base of the hopper, down the tube, and into the newly-created hole.

With jittering steps, the spider-box crept forward and repeated its dance. *Yes! It's working! It's planting the rice field!*

But her joy was short lived, as one of the legs took a turn to one side. The entire mechanism tilted and careened sideways with a splash, spilling the remaining seeds into the water. And not incidentally splattering her with mud.

Sighing, she retrieved what was now her latest in a long string of failed attempts to create a rice-planting machine. As she had done so many times before, she stuffed the soggy box back into her bag and began the long trek back to Hamarata Castle. She would have to sneak back into her quarters again and prepare for a short night of little sleep knowing her project was still no closer to success.

The light of dawn seemingly erupted into Miako's room. She groaned; it felt like she had just fallen asleep moments ago…

"Lady Miako! You must awaken now!"

The voice was that of Shensha, her elderly maid, who was also responsible for the sudden opening of the rice paper screen over the window.

Miako turned away from the light. "Let me sleep just a little longer, Shensha…" she mumbled.

"Up now, Lady, not a day for dallying. Big things afoot." There was an unusual note of worry in her voice.

Miako sat up, about to ask what was wrong, when a deep rumbling sound answered the question for her. It echoed around the chamber, over and over.

The war drums of Hamarata sounded.

After dressing quickly, Miako hurried down the corridor, Shensha scurried behind her vainly trying to keep up. The highly polished wood floors thrummed with the sound of many feet as servants and samurai dashed everywhere. The continuing beat of the war drums brought looks of worry to every face.

As the pair reached the audience chamber, the kneeling door servant slid open the rice paper door for the daimyo's daughter. Miako entered, her maid taking her station outside with the other staff.

Her father, the daimyo and ruler of Hamarata, was already seated on the ceremonial stool. Her brothers and the elders of the clan knelt on the floor to either side. Miako quickly found her place beside her mother at the back of the room. With a practiced grace that belied her own nervousness, she parted the folds of her kimono so that she could kneel down on one of the cushions reserved for the ladies of the court.

"The war has finally come to us," her father was saying. "The Yama Obake, our ancestral spirits of the mountain, have protected us thus far from the great battles between Shogun and Emperor. But the conflict is fluid, the factions each seeking the best battlefield for their advantage. Alas it appears that their chosen battlefield will soon be here, on our mountain."

Miako glanced around the room. The gloomy expressions, and not a few looks of fear, made her shiver.

"We know," her father continued, "that a priority for both sides will be our castle, for whoever claims it will hold an advantage. Hamarata has always been a neutral province. If we submit to either side, the other will then try to destroy us. Thus we have no choice but to prepare the war machines to defend ourselves. The Baths are to be shut down, and all of the Joki is to be channeled to the great guns."

This elicited a round of murmuring, for the Joki, the intricate network of pipes that fed the heated steam from under the mountain to the many community baths and hot water springs, was the economic mainstay of Hamarata. Between the war coming to their lands, and the shutting down of the springs, it would bring unimaginable hardship to everyone.

Her father stood and everyone in the room bowed forehead to floor. He let the silence hang for a moment. "May the Yama Obake look over us and protect our mountain." As he strode from the room, his retainers got to their feet and hurried to their posts. Miako looked to her mother for guidance but as always, that was the wrong place to look for any such thing.

"What will we do, what will we do?" her mother wailed. The senior lady's maid dashed in from the corridor and helped her mother to her feet, comforting her on the way back to the women's quarters.

When Shensha arrived Miako waved her maid away. "I am fine, really. Please, go assist with my mother." Nodding dutifully, Shensha padded after the others.

Miako rose and settled her kimono around her. She had someplace much more important to be.

The bustling of servants and retainers made it easier than usual for Miako to make her way across the courtyard to the steam house without someone wondering what the daimyo's daughter was doing anywhere near such a place. The noble women were presumed to always be in the state chambers, or working on calligraphy, or perhaps practicing their koto playing. As she reached the stout wooden door to the steam house, she unhooked the iron latch, slipped inside quickly, and pulled the door closed behind her.

It was cool and dim inside, the only light filtered up from the tunnel of stone steps descending in front of her. The gentle hiss of steam likewise rose, along with the wafting odor of warm grease. Despite this place being absolutely forbidden to her, she found comfort here.

She lifted up the hem of her kimono, careful lest it gather any incriminating dirt or oil residue and descended into the earth's embrace.

Brass lanterns hanging from hooks on the stone-lined walls cast a dim glow across the control chamber as she entered. The maze of pipes and valves in this subterranean cavern had scared her the first time she had snuck down here, their glistening metal seeming to perspire like a farmer working under the summer sun. Yet the tongue-lashing she had received from Tomaratu had scared her even more. Completely blind, the old man who tended the Joki hadn't had a clue who had invaded his private sanctuary, nor did he care. "What damn fool let you down here?" he had growled at her. For even though she had not spoken a word, he had heard her footfalls even over the hiss of the steaming pipes. "Get your arse back up into the light and leave me be."

That first day she had indeed scampered back up the steps to the safety of her rooms. Yet the sense of power in that chamber, the pulse of the steam, the very rawness of it all, drew her back. Up above ground, with all the court rituals, the springs and baths were cloaked in mystique and ceremonies of purity. Yet the rituals obscured the reality of what made the waters of the baths soothing and warm in the first place. The essence of the Joki, the steam which gave it life, was down here below the mountain. And Tomaratu was the Joki's keeper.

Well, keeper was not entirely correct. While his decades of knowledge, by touch alone, allowed him to turn this valve or that lever just the tiniest amount to keep the flow of steam exactly so, he was the first to say —

"Are you here again, scamp? Wretched girl, disturbing my harmony…"

She smiled as he emerged from behind one of the stands of pipes. She had grown to love that irascible voice, which had snapped and snarled even after he had discovered who she was. In fact, he probably growled at her more because of it.

"Yes, Master Tomaratu, it's Miako."

"I've told you, girl, I'm not no master," he admonished her as he heaved his scrawny weight against a large metal lever on what she now knew to be the main condenser. "This ain't no shrine. This is working things, not make-believe foolishness."

"I know, Mas- um, Tomaratu. But aren't you the one who always tells me that the Yama Obake spirits are the ones who provide the mountain's essence?"

Tomaratu ceased pushing on the metal bar, his body language conveying that he felt sufficient leverage had at last been achieved. "True enough. But that be wholly different than that foolery people do above. The mountain kami are true; they are here —" as he placed a hand against the stone wall, "all our ancestors… They care for us all." He turned with a snort, shuffling down the rows of gauges, their glass fronts removed so that he could feel their needles with his fingertips. "All those puffed-up people above know nothing about that, sitting on their naked arses in the springs the kami warm for them."

Miako followed him, observing carefully everything he did. It was he, in his gruff but tolerant manner, who had taught her the ways of the Yama Obake: how the heat flowed from below the mountain to the chambers here, where it was all converted into incredibly hot steam and thence piped to all the springs around Hamarata. And it was he who had taught her how to make things; things that would horrify her mother should she learn of them. Noble women were not supposed to even acknowledge the existence of low-born workmen like Tomaratu, let alone spend time in their company.

For his part, the old man had wanted nothing to do with her either but her persistence in returning in spite of his remonstrations, coupled with her penchant for learning, had gradually loosened his tongue. She discovered that behind the glowering visage lay a patient teacher.

Tomaratu stopped at one particular gauge, turning his head slightly in the way she knew meant he had heard something that was not right. "I suppose your silly rice-planting toy failed again, eh?"

Embarrassed, she nodded before remembering he could not see that. "Yes, it fell over again. But that was not why I came down today."

Tomaratu turned in her direction. His coarse voice was unusually soft. "What be troubling you, girl?"

For a blind man who worked only with his hands, she found him amazingly perceptive. "I am scared, Tomaratu. The war is coming here, to Hamarata. The drums have sounded, and all the men are preparing for war."

He nodded solemnly. "Figured so. Could hear those blasted drums even down here."

Miako touched one of the knobs for the pipe that sent water up to the women's quarters where she enjoyed her hot bath every morning. "I know the Joki has been here for ages, but... I am worried that all of this could be lost, if cannons and steam muskets are let loose on Hamarata."

Tomaratu made the tiniest of adjustments to a valve. "Do not fret, girl. The Yama Obake will protect their mountain, and us, their children." Then he turned away with a deep sigh.

While she heard his reassuring words, it was the sigh that stayed with her.

As the armies of the Shogun and of the Emperor approached from the east and the west, converging on Hamarata, the castle's great war cannons were trundled into position just behind the parapets. Miako watched from the window of her quarters high in the central tower keep. As each machine was wheeled into place, soldiers hooked it up to the flexible bamboo piping that was attached at the other end to the Joki system. The power of the mountain was being taken from the warm and gentle baths and channeled to the war machines, a thought that made Miako cringe. Even so, the part of her that was fascinated with the mechanisms below allowed her to grasp the working of the weapons as the soldiers ran through a practice shot.

There was a large metal tank at the rear of the cannon, and while the pressure within it built, a soldier carefully placed an iron ball at the very end of the muzzle. A small, hinged door was open on the surface of the ball, from which protruded a long fuse. At a signal from the gun captain, everything happened very quickly. The soldier stuffed most of the fuse down into the opening, lit the end, and closed the little door tight over it; then other soldiers tilted the cannon back until it pointed over the parapet. The gun captain heaved on a stout lever at the rear of the pressure vessel, and everyone covered their ears.

An enormous BOOM shook even the tower from which Miako watched. The ball was flung from the cannon: barely visible, it arced across the sky before landing in one of the now-abandoned fields before the castle. An instant later there was a huge flash and a column of dirt spewed upward as another rumbling boom echoed back to the castle.

As the soldiers fed more steam into the cannon, Miako looked up to the mountain behind the castle. What would the Yama Obake think about how the essence of their mountain was being used?

"When this war is all said and done, what next?" Tomaratu's voice echoed down to Miako. She had arrived in the control room to find nothing but his bare feet visible where he stood on a rickety wooden ladder, the rest of him hidden up among a nest of overflow piping. "Rice plantin', that's what. Always been, always will be. People need rice. Nobody needs fancy baths."

He came down, slowly and deliberately, making sure of his footing with each step. "And you know a little something about both rice plantin' and steam, I figure." He alighted beside her, wiping his hands on his grimy tunic. "Had to stop a leak from spreading up there, keep the flow going the way it ought."

Miako's worries right now, though, were not about the pipes or the rice paddies but the armies that would trample those paddies and farm fields just beyond the walls. "But Tomaratu, if Hamarata is burned to the ground by all the fighting, there will not be any rice seeds left to plant. Nor any people to till them."

The old man grunted. "You told me that afore you came down here today, you looked up to the mountain. Thought about the kami. You think they ain't seen wars before? They been around for centuries. Mountain even longer than that. Now, you look at that mountain, how big it is. Then you look at all them angry ants waving their little sticks down below." He shook his head. "Mountain ain't worried about all that. Neither you be." The last word was cut off by a sharp fit of coughing, forcing him to double over.

Alarmed, she took hold of his arm. "Tomaratu! Are you alright?"

He waved her off. "Fine, I be fine." He started a slow shuffle over to his threadbare cot, in a little cubbyhole carved out of the side of the chamber. "Just needs to sit a spell, is all." But he nearly collapsed as he fell down onto the cot, his breathing now heavy.

Armies and fighting fled her mind as she stooped to lift his legs onto the cot, trying to get him comfortable. "I will fetch the court physician!"

Again he waved her off. "Don't bother with that, girl. People up there needing a lot more tending than me, right soon." He coughed, a deep hacking sound that echoed off the walls. "Bodies be like pipes, now and then they wears out and needs replacing and I reckon that the same with me now."

"But who could replace you, Tomaratu? You've always been a part of the Joki, you know where every pipe goes, what every valve does."

He just smiled again. "The mountain will provide," was all he would say.

As the armies approached, it seemed that all of the people of the province had tried to cram into the castle. Miako and the noble women opened their chambers to accommodate women and children, while the farmers and trades people were handed weapons and sent to assist the soldiers manning the walls.

A group of excitable ladies stood at Miako's window, and she tried to peer around them to see what had drawn their attention. Once she got a clear view, her heart sank.

In what had once been the verdant green farmland now amassed legions of war machines, having been positioned during the night, their movements hidden in the darkness. The large swath of blue-hued uniforms to the east were the Shogun's forces, while those in red and black to the west belonged to the emperor. Color aside, there was not much to distinguish them: both sides had row upon row of massive steam cannons, much larger than Hamarata's. Lacking the natural energy of a mountain, each cannon was tended by a cart with its own boiler, fed from supply wagons at the rear heaped with firewood for the burners heating the water into steam.

Arrayed between the cannons were great crossbows, machines with racks and racks of arrows in hoppers on top, like an infernal version of her rice planter. The contraptions were hooked up to the boilers powering the cannons, using their energy to propel their deadly darts. She had read of these machines, that could loose a bolt, retract, reload, and fire another, over and over until the sky hung black with arrows.

She saw groups from each army break off to approach the castle. She knew they would want this high ground for their own, to fire weapons down below onto their enemies, and to control their forces from its lofty vantage.

The day she had been dreading had arrived. Pushing herself away from the window, Miako hurried down the stairs to warn Tomaratu.

She did not get very far. A soldier was stationed at the entrance to the steam room stairwell. He bowed to her as she approached but did not move aside. "Your pardon, Lady Miako, but no one is allowed inside, per orders of the daimyo." He explained that the Joki was now under the control of the army, to supply the war machines.

Miako could care less about the war machines, or the war. Her immediate concern was for the ailing Tomaratu. At her explanation, the soldier was surprised. "That crazy old fellow down below? He died during the night."

The coarse, unfeeling words washed past her in a blur. Tomaratu was *gone*? The keeper of the Joki, who had dedicated his entire life to tending the Yama Obake? It was more than her heart could bear.

Trudging back up to her crowded chambers, she didn't hear the shouting of the soldiers on the wall, nor the crack of muskets or their peculiar whistle as their steam percussion hammers re-charged before firing another round. Even the massive boom of the steam cannon on the parapets, lobbing their explosive charges onto the heads of the competing invaders down below, failed to register in her mind.

Tomaratu was no more. And it seemed that soon the mountain springs, and with it the Yama Obake, also would be no more.

All that day, smoke and fire raged on the fields below the castle, as the firing of cannons and muskets, and the screams of the dying, echoed back and forth between the armies. Evenly matched, neither side could force the other back.

The women sat far away from the now heavily-shuttered windows in the keep. All could hear the impact of musket balls on the stone and wood, and all cringed whenever a cannon was set off down below, never sure if one of the great exploding balls would land on their refuge. But the armies wanted to use the castle towers, not destroy them, or so they told themselves. Miako barely listened to any of the frenzied speculation. All she could think about was the loss of her friend, her mentor, and her guide to the Joki and the Yama Obake.

A particularly large detonation nearby shook the entire tower, setting off another round of wailing from the assembled women. But one young woman in their midst wept for the mountain and the death and destruction that had been brought to it.

As night fell, the battle subsided. Both sides retreated to their lines, leaving the field between them strewn with the dead. The heavy shutters of the tower had been opened with the coming of darkness, allowing the stuffy air inside to escape, but also letting in the fetid smells of death from below.

Nevertheless, Miako sat next to the window, the same one she had gazed from since she was a child. Back then she would try to count the stars until she grew sleepy and nodded off. To distract herself from the pain in her heart, she began counting again. Gradually, the groans of wounded men and sobs of distraught women faded as she focused on each pinpoint of light.

Quite to her surprise, the clouds in the night sky seemed to move, twisting and turning. *How odd; there is no breeze, what is making them do that?*

The clouds slid gracefully down toward the ground and back up again, in a fluid, majestic spiral… right toward her window! Startled, she watched as they coalesced, taking vaguely… *human* shapes! Dozens of them, arrayed in mid-air just outside her window!

Two of the nearest ones extended ethereal hands, silently beckoning to her. Tentatively, she reached out, touching their misty forms… and she let out a little yelp as her feet rose off the floor. Yet the movement was graceful and slow. With infinite patience, the Yama Obake gently embraced and encircled her, guiding her up and out through the window!

Far below, the ground still smoldered with the fires of spent munitions and the remains of trees and shrubs. She ought to have been terrified to be flying up into the sky, and yet… she felt oddly at peace.

Surrounding her like a bevy of doting relatives, the ethereal kami flew her out across the mountainside, ever higher. Up here the air was chill, the sky clear of any fire smoke. She saw the moonlight, Tsukiyomi's moonlight, glittering off the bits of snow still atop the peak.

Onward they went, soft gentle turns down and around the mountain… As they passed over each of the now-abandoned Hamarata baths they paused, and one or the other of the kami would whisper inside her head: *"This one I made, back so many, many years ago… Have you been to this one? You have? I am so proud!… Oh, I had the hardest time here, the rock was so thick…"*

After what seemed hours, and yet almost no time at all, they arrived back over the castle… directly over the steam house. One of the voices, which somehow felt as if it spoke for them all, entered her mind. *"Little one, you have seen our creations… and you know what binds them."*

She nodded, not needing to speak, for they already knew her thoughts…

"Yes… the Joki connect them all… just as blood flows through you, so the essence of the mountain flows through them. What you cannot see, below the ground, is where it all flows to the metal pipes of the Joki…"

An image came into her mind… a vast underground reservoir of water extending in an arc all around the mountain, around Hamarata castle… with the pipes of the Joki between it and the heat generated from deep below, the two combining to create the baths… the pressure of that combination constrained by the pipes. And that if that pressure was released…

She felt the concurrence of the kami. *"The springs were our creation for the children who came after us. Now those springs must be used to save those children from destruction. Throughout all time, nothing stays immutable. The mountain gives to us all, and new generations must find their own paths, their own creations."*

With a heart heavy in understanding, Miako knew what must be done.

A sudden noise startled her awake. Her shoulders were cramped, as she had apparently fallen asleep leaning against the windowsill.

The noise was the sound of muskets, the shouts of men — it was dawn! And the fighting had begun again.

Everything was in an uproar as Miako was hurriedly pulled away from the open window and the heavy wooden shutter lowered back in place, none too soon as musket balls thudded into the wood a moment later.

Miako slipped out of the tower room and down the stairs. She peered out across the main courtyard toward the entrance to the steam room. Fortunately, the guard was no longer there — she presumed gone to the walls to help in the defense. The door stood open, the bamboo pipes that fed the war machines snaking their way from it across the courtyard toward the walls, channeling the mountain's life blood.

Wasting no time, she dashed for the steam room door and hurried down the stone stairs. The Joki chamber enveloped her in its familiar smell of steam and grease. Even below ground she could hear the thud of the cannon above. All around her, she could see the pipes from the courtyard patched into the valves of the Joki.

She had to hurry; once she started the process it would not take long for those above ground to realize something was amiss. She ran to the far end of the line of valves, and worked her way back toward the stairs, grabbing each handle in turn to rotate the valve to reroute the steam from the war machine conduits back into the main Joki pipes. And each Joki valve she spun up to full pressure, evoking the name of the Yama Obake as she did so.

The sound of hissing steam turned into a roar, yet still she hurried down the line of valves, turning every single one fully open. The noise was almost unbearable, and her hands burned from the heat, but she did not stop. She knew that all of the baths above, and the reservoir below the mountain, would soon froth with superheated water.

Just as she got to the stairs, one of the nearby pipes burst, sending scalding steam right at her. Something seemed to grab hold of her and yank her back, deep into the stair passage. She looked down and thought she could see a pair of ethereal arms wrapped around her. Behind her she was certain she saw the ghostly face of Tomaratu… and at that moment a massive explosion, and another, and another, blotted out all sound as she lost consciousness.

Miako's head was spinning and there was a massive ringing in her ears. She choked on dust, rolling over onto her stomach where she lay on the ground. Her eyes stung from the smoke and dust but she was able to see that she lay in the courtyard, not far from the steam room entrance. The remains of the war machine piping were all entangled around and near her.

The sound of cannons and gunfire had ceased. She looked around, worried that Hamarata had already fallen, but no one was nearby. Gazing upward, she saw that everyone, the nobility, warriors, and servants alike, stood atop the walls, looking out toward the battlefield.

Staggering to her feet, her clothes dirty and torn, a bleeding gash on her cheek, she climbed up the wall steps to join them, peering over... and saw a massive moat of scalding, steaming water, completely surrounding them on all sides.

All of the springs, and the reservoir, had erupted in that massive explosion. The smoke and steam partly blocked the view beyond, but she could see that both invading armies now fled from the field, leaving their war machines behind.

Haramata now stood within a new moat, and the invasion seemed to be over. The power of the Yama Obake had spoken, and the little ants with their sticks knew they were no match for the spirits of the mountain.

"What will we do? Everything has been lost!" Miako's mother cried out, wailing about the loss of the baths and hot springs, the source of their wealth and prestige.

Miako looked down upon the abandoned war machines and recalled Tomaratu's words to her: *"You know a little something about both rice plantin' and steam, I figure."* In an instant, she realized the possibilities. The arrow machines were not unlike her little rice planting spider, only much larger. Replace the arrow hopper with a seed hopper, and alter the bolt-throwing mechanism to point downward and make a planting hole... and use the boilers from the steam cannon to power it all... Would articulated legs be able to move it? The war cannons were pulled along on a set of wheels, so maybe the *steam* could roll the wheels...

She spoke quietly, but without hesitation. "I know *exactly* what we must do."

No Safe Harbour

Aaron Rosenberg

Phillipe Huron, Detective-Inspector for la Préfecture de Police de Paris, stepped out of the airship to find waiting for him a frowning foreign officer, a pressing case, and a powerful fragrance wafting from a city the likes of which he had never seen. Taking a moment to adjust his collar, resettle his hat, and shift his shoulders to accommodate Detective Dupin's weight upon the right side, he used that time to absorb that first view of fabled Hong Kong.

Known as the "fragrant harbour" and one of the biggest, most active ports in all the world, Phillipe had expected the hustle and bustle, with all its attendant noises and smells. Nor was he disappointed. Everywhere he looked, people charged to and fro, carting this or that, ferrying customers to and from, or simply rushing to one berth or another to begin, continue, or conclude some business. The fact that only a handful of suits were in evidence and a great many wore a simple shirt or tunic over loose pants, silk being prevalent over wool or even linen and cotton, would take some getting used to, and he could already see that he would stand out in his standard French garb. But it was more that the air was thick with the scent of spices and herbs rather than oil and metal that most surprised him.

Stretching out before him, high above the mist-shrouded ground but still below the mooring towers themselves, Hong Kong looked like something out of a fairy tale. The buildings were all faceted layers, each level smaller than the one below it and each with a tiled roof that flared out at the edges. Gracefully arched bridges connected one building to another, forming a latticework as far as the eye could see. Handsomely carved wooden screens covered each window, allowing privacy without blocking light or air. Spherical paper lanterns hung from lintels and silk streamers from columns, giving the whole a festive air.

"Pretty!" Dupin squawked from his perch. "Flowers!"

"Yes, it does smell like flowers, doesn't it?" Phillipe agreed, reaching up to stroke his companion's glossy black feathers. The airship attendant was quietly glaring behind him, however, so he let himself be ushered down the ramp and toward the man waiting patiently there.

"Inspector Huron?" His welcoming committee of one's pronunciation was regrettably bad, and Phillipe was relieved when the man switched to English — though heavily accented, that was a good deal more understandable. "I am Inspector Wu Siong. I have been appointed by the Ministry to assist you in your endeavors here." The inspector was not terribly tall, which made him seem particularly short against Phillipe's own lanky frame, and it was difficult to tell his build beneath the long, high-collared black silk coat he wore buttoned down to his knees, but his face was rounded, with few lines, and the thick braid of hair beneath his cap hung like a glossy black rope down his back.

Phillipe returned the man's bow, Dupin automatically shifting weight to compensate. "Inspector Siong, thank you. I look forward to working with you."

He thought he saw a grimace cross the other man's face, if only for an instant. "Here in China, we place our family names first," he explained carefully. "Thus I am known as Inspector Wu."

"Ah. My apologies. It is my first trip to your nation." Dupin cawed, flapping his wings, and Wu flinched a bit. "And I'm sorry about Detective Dupin, here. He does not enjoy long flights."

"Of course." Wu did not glance at the bird. "How do you wish to proceed? We have taken the liberty of securing you a room at one of our finest hotels. Would you like to refresh yourself there?"

Phillipe shook his head. "No, if it's all right with you I'd prefer to get started right away. The longer we wait, the colder the trail gets."

Wu dipped his head. "Certainly. Please follow me." And, turning, he led the way along the row of towers that made up Hong Kong's airship docks.

With his longer stride and less-restrictive outerwear, Phillipe easily kept pace with his guide. "What do we know about Chapdelaine so far?" he asked as they walked, passing one set of iron struts after another. This much, at least, looked familiar to him!

The local inspector's face showed no expression as he recited: "Father Auguste Chapdelaine arrived from Paris by the airship *Lumiere* on May 7, 1852, which was four days ago. He has not been seen or heard from since."

Phillipe nodded. That matched the sparse details he'd been given by Prefect Lepine before being rushed here. "Chapdelaine was a parochial vicar," he explained to his companion. "He was in charge of a small town called Boucey. We know that he left there on April 29 by way of a postal ship to Paris, and from there boarded the *Lumiere*. We have no idea why, however." The Catholic Church had alerted the police when the priest had gone missing, and when they found out he'd left the country Phillipe had been ordered to go after him. Of course, he was not entirely sure why a single priest abandoning his post mattered so much that they'd felt the need to send him all the way here, but he had his orders.

They paused by one of the mooring towers, and he leaned back, craning his neck to study the airship there. The French flag was proudly displayed along its sides. "That is the *Lumiere?*"

Wu nodded. "I have already spoken with the captain," he warned. "He has been less than forthcoming."

"I'll try my luck anyway," Phillipe said with a small smile. He received no such expression in return. It was like working with a statue! Setting the thought aside, Phillipe pressed the Call button at the tower's base.

"Yes?" a voice replied a moment later, the English laced with a familiar accent.

"Bonjour," he answered in French. "Am I speaking with the captain of *la Lumiere?*"

"Oui," the man said, already sounding less guarded. "Capitaine Andre Durand. And who am I speaking with?"

"This is Inspector Phillipe Huron of la PP," he answered, using the force's familiar nickname only a fellow Parisian—or one who did frequent business there—would know. "I would like to ask you about one of your recent passengers. May I come up?"

There was a buzz and a click as the tower's door unlocked. Phillipe pulled it open, stepping into the small, mesh-sided cage within. After a second, Wu joined him. Closing the door again, he engaged the mechanism and they both waited as the compartment carried them up to the ship.

Captain Durand was a short, stout man with the weathered skin and bowlegged gait of a lifelong sailor, whether by sea or by air. He scowled at Wu but nodded at Phillipe when they were escorted to the bridge.

"You're Paris Police?" Durand asked warily, and grunted upon examining Phillipe's identity card. "Long way from home."

"I am, yes. I understand you arrived four days ago from Paris, is that correct? And that one of your passengers was a priest named Chapdelaine?"

Durand jerked his chin toward Wu, who waited patiently a step behind. "Already told this one as much."

Phillipe carefully shifted so that the captain's eyes were wholly upon him. "Please," he said. "Father Chapdelaine abandoned his parish without a word of explanation. We believe he may be in distress. I have been sent to find him and make sure he is hale and hearty."

The airship captain unbent slightly, if only to scoff. "In distress? Not likely! Papa Chapdelaine—that's what he insisted everyone call him—was a model passenger. Polite, friendly, and excited. Said he'd never been on a long-range ship before. Never left France before, neither. He couldn't wait to get here."

Dupin squawked and fluttered his wings, echoing Phillipe's own confusion. "Do you know where he was headed once he arrived?" he asked. "Was he meeting with someone?" Perhaps he'd had an urgent call for help from a former parishioner, though it seemed unlikely.

Durand shook his head. "No idea. Some of the crew might know, though. Like I said, he talked to everybody." The captain frowned. "You think he's in trouble?"

"I don't know," Phillipe admitted. "But I was sent to find out."

He thanked the captain and turned to go. They could ask each of the crew in turn, of course, but an airship this size had scores of sailors, maybe as many as a hundred. Going through them all would take a great deal of time, and he was already four days behind his quarry.

As they left the bridge, Wu sidled up alongside him. "That man there, with the golden hair," he said quietly, and Phillipe followed the inspector's gaze toward a sailor with blond curls. "He looked away when the captain suggested speaking to the crew."

Phillipe favored his local counterpart with a smile. "Good eye." Then he confronted the sailor in question. "Excuse me. Did you know Papa Chapdelaine?"

The sailor started, glancing this way and that, but finally met Phillipe's glance. "Aye. Seemed a decent sort. No fancy airs about him."

"And might you know where he was headed from here? He may need help," Phillipe added when the sailor hesitated.

That seemed to decide him. "I directed him toward a boarding house," the blond man admitted. "Shoo geh how jewey."

Wu stared. "Why would you send him there in particular?" Even though his face remained neutral, Phillipe caught a note of disapproval in the local inspector's voice.

The sailor must have heard it as well, because he bristled, straightening to glare down at Wu. "He asked! He had it written down already!"

"Thank you," Phillipe told him, stepping between them. "I appreciate your help."

Turning away, he put a hand on Wu's shoulder and guided the man from the ship. "You know the place he mentioned?" he asked only after they'd exited the mooring tower and were back on the docks.

Wu nodded. "Shuì gè hǎo jué," he repeated, the words sliding gracefully from his lips. "It means 'good sleep.' It is not the sort of place affluent travelers would visit."

"Yet Chapdelaine knew it by name," Phillipe mused. "How, when he'd never even left France before?" He shook his head. "Well, at least we know our next stop."

This time his guide wore a definite frown. "Yes. But you must prepare yourself for a side of the city few visitors are permitted to see."

That intrigued Phillipe almost as much as this case was beginning to, and he gestured for his companion to lead the way.

Wu took them down a narrow staircase from the docks, descending into and through the mist that seemed to blanket the entire city — and below that, Phillipe discovered a whole new world hidden beneath the first.

The buildings here were big and squared, made of sturdy and unadorned stone. Bamboo blinds covered large windows and signs above doorways proclaimed businesses in Chinese characters. The heavy aroma of spices still scented the air, but the flowery notes had been replaced by the stink of garbage, cooking oil, and human sweat. People thronged the dirt streets, pushing and shoving in both directions, with almost everyone dressed in loose local clothing. Phillipe caught sight of one or two other Europeans in the crowd, but they were in the conspicuous minority.

"The upper level is for travelers, traders, merchants," Wu explained, threading his way through the crowd with practiced ease. Phillipe struggled to keep up. "Here is where we live and work." He made a small sound that might have been displeasure. "Certain officials felt it best to keep this side of things hidden. They devised an electrical grid to prevent the steam's passage, spreading it between here and the upper level instead. Most visitors never know any of this is here."

"Is that why you were displeased about the boarding house?" Phillipe asked his guide, having to shout to be heard over the constant din of so many people. "Because it's essentially belowstairs?"

His fellow officer nodded. "I know of the place by name and reputation," he answered over his shoulder. "It is not the worst, but far from the best, even down here."

They came to a side street and Wu turned down it, then had to reach back and grab Phillipe by the wrist to drag him through the foot traffic. Dupin flared his wings at the sudden change in direction, and all around them people muttered and backed away, giving them space for the first time.

"Wūyā," Wu explained, nodding toward the crow. "They are ill omens. People are afraid. A man with such on his shoulder, he brings misfortune."

"Only for those who deserve it," Phillipe promised, stroking Dupin's feathers to settle the bird. Still, he appreciated the reaction his friend had caused, as it made their passage easier.

Another turn or two, and finally Wu stopped before a building no different from its neighbors. "Here," he said, pointing at its placard. "Shuì gè hǎo jué. I will do the speaking." It was somewhere between a demand and a request, but Phillipe was only too happy to accede. He followed the Chinese inspector into the building but hung back to listen and observe.

The entryway was tall but narrow, lit only by a single naked bulb overhead, and smelled of rice, stewed meat, and harsh soap. At the far end a wide desk blocked a carved door, behind which rose a steep staircase. An older Chinese woman sat behind the desk, eyeing them as they approached.

Wu had been the soul of politeness and mild manners up to this point, but now Phillipe saw a new version of his guide. The man's steps were firm, his stance upright, and his tone when he spoke was sharp and authoritative. The woman's eyes widened slightly but she quickly lowered them as she bowed deeply. When she answered, her own voice was soft, hesitant, and fully compliant.

After a moment, Wu glanced back and gestured for Phillipe to join him. "This is Madame Chung," he explained. "The proprietress. She confirms that yes, your priest was here. He departed two days ago, however."

Phillipe bit back a grimace. Two days ago! He had already been en route himself by then, the journey from Paris taking three days. If only he'd left sooner, he might have caught Chapdelaine here and saved himself further trouble!

"May we see his room?" he asked Wu, who translated the request—in what sounded like nonnegotiable terms—to Madame Chung. A few minutes later they were hiking up the long stair behind her.

"She has not yet had it cleaned," Wu explained as the woman brought them down a tight corridor, stopped at one door, and unlocked it for them with a heavy iron key.

Stepping inside, Phillipe saw a small, plain room, little more than a cell, though at least it shared a window on the far wall with its neighbors. A low bed occupied all of one side, while the other held a small, rickety dresser and a little table. Other than those pieces and the accompanying bed linens, plus a pitcher and basin on the dresser, the room was bare.

"Does she have any idea where he might have gone?" he asked, but Wu shook his head.

"She does not. This is not the sort of place where one would ask. He paid for two nights when he arrived, however."

Phillipe considered that. "So he planned to leave here when he did. The question is, where was he going next? And why?" None of it made any sense to him, but at least it did not sound as if Chapdelaine had been forced into anything.

Exiting the boarding house, Phillipe studied the street and immediately saw what he wanted. "There," he said, pointing across the way at a second-floor balcony. An old man sat there, smoking a pipe and watching them.

Wu was quick to catch on. "Wait here," he instructed, and cut through the traffic, disappearing into the building beyond. A moment later Phillipe saw the old man glance behind him, then get up and vanish inside. He returned with Wu, and the two stood there speaking for a bit before the inspector bowed and left.

"Your instinct was correct," Wu said when he rejoined Phillipe on the street soon after. "Mister Tsai sits there every day, smoking and reading the paper and watching his neighbors come and go. He saw your priest arrive on the seventh — and saw him depart two days ago, on the ninth. Nor was he alone." The frown had returned. "He was accompanied by two men, both foreigners. Tsai did not know them, or hear their conversation — but he did notice something else. A certain look in their eyes. Dreamy and disconnected."

Phillipe knew at once what his counterpart meant. "Opium." The drug had made its way to France, though they had done their best to stamp it out, but he knew it was rampant here.

Wu nodded. "Yes. And for a foreigner wishing to partake here below the mist, there is only one place to go. The Lucky Dragon."

Phillipe had no idea what to expect from the Lucky Dragon. He was not prepared, however, when they entered the building Wu selected after several blocks, to find a wide, pleasant room with painted screens on the walls, silk draperies covering the low ceiling, rich rugs on the floor, and hanging lanterns illuminating cozy nooks made up of low couches with small, ornately carved wooden tables beside them. The air hung thick with smoke, some of it tobacco by the scent but he also detected notes of amber, wood, and something sweet he assumed must be the drug itself. People lounged on several of the couches, all of them fellow foreigners by their garb and their coloring, and Chinese attendants moved to and fro, carrying trays with pitchers, pots, cups, small plates of food, little bowls, and long, thin pipes.

A woman moved to greet them as the door swung shut behind, cutting off the mist-filtered daylight. She was young and pretty, and wore a bright-red silk dress patterned with white flowers, its collar high but its sleeves short enough to leave most of her toned arms bare and its fit tight enough to display her curves. "Hello, and welcome to the

Lucky Dragon!" she said in excellent English, her bright gaze focused entirely on Phillipe. "Is this your first time with us?"

Wu cut her off with a sharp bark of Chinese and she froze, the smile falling from her lips as his words brought instant compliance. She hurried away, returning a moment later trailing behind an older, wider, but still handsome woman in a more European-style dress of dark blue silk.

"This is Madame Li Rui," Wu stated, dipping his head to her ever so slightly. "The owner. She will answer your questions."

Phillipe bowed. "Madame Li, it is a pleasure. I am seeking a man I believe was here recently, a Catholic priest named Auguste Chapdelaine. He would have arrived two days ago."

She nodded, with a wary glance at Wu. "Yes, I remember him well." Her English was nearly as good as the younger woman's, and her eyes were far sharper. "He came in with two friends, but would not partake himself. They did. They are well known here."

He waited, but when she did not elaborate, he was forced to ask, "Do you know their names?"

The proprietress started to shake her head, but Wu frowned and the motion died at once. "Dennis and Christopher," she admitted finally. "That is all we know them as."

"Are they still here?" He had dared to hope, but that died with her response.

"No. They left just before noon." It was only an hour or two past that now, and Phillipe repressed the urge to scream. So close!

Instead he asked, "Where did they sit?" Perhaps someone had seen something useful.

Madame Li turned to the girl, who bowed. "Follow me, please." And she stepped out onto the main floor, winding between couches to a handful arranged in the back corner. "They were here."

A man lay on one of the couches there, and Phillipe regarded him at once. European, certainly, of middle age, and most likely affluent given the cut of his suit, but his face was flushed, his jaw and cheeks slack, his eyes half closed. One of the pipes lay across his chest. "Excuse me?" Phillipe tried anyway, and after a second the man blinked up at him.

"Ah." A dreamy smile crossed his face. "What a splendid bird." Dupin preened at the compliment.

"You are English?" Phillipe judged from the man's accent, and was pleased when he nodded. "The men who were here, did you know them?" A shake. "Did you speak with them? The priest?"

"Oh." Now the stranger's eyes focused a little more. "Yes. Very kind. Very excited to begin his work."

Phillipe frowned, bending down to hear better. "His work?"

"Yes." Each word emerged so slowly, like a soap bubble, drifting up from the man's daze. "Missionary work. Very noble."

Now *that* was interesting! "Did he say where he would be doing this work?"

But he got no reply. The man had slipped into sleep, or something much like it.

Still, as they left Phillipe felt a small thrill. Finally, a clue!

Not sure where to go next, he agreed to Wu's suggestion that they eat something. That turned out to mean visiting a small shop in the area, where they were seated at a quiet table near the back of the cramped interior and brought large bowls of steaming, fragrant soup, filled with long noodles, shredded pork, and various unfamiliar vegetables. Still, it smelled amazing, and Phillipe discovered he was famished, devoting himself to slurping up the noodles, spooning up the meat, vegetables, and broth, and washing it all down with small cups of hot, faintly floral tea.

When they'd both sated their appetites, he sat back and let Dupin peck at the remains as he puzzled things out. "Chapdelaine was not kidnapped or forced, or even coerced," he stated after a moment. "He is here as a missionary."

Wu nodded. He had cleaned his entire bowl in short order. "Others have come as such. But they are rarely welcome."

"The problem," Phillipe explained, "is that he isn't a missionary. Those have to be approved by the bishop, and it was he who contacted us to say that Chapdelaine had gone missing. So someone is lying, or at least mistaken."

"It would help if we knew where he was planning to go next," Wu put in. "Much of my country does not like Catholics, but there are parts where he would be greeted with outright violence."

Phillipe considered that. "Does someone wish him ill, then? This seems an odd and roundabout way to cause him harm. Why go to all the trouble?"

His companion frowned, toying with the pair of cylindrical sticks he'd dexterously used to eat his food. "Perhaps it is not him that is the target. There are enough tensions between our two nations already."

That was certainly true enough. Though it was Britain and China who had the most contention, France was more and more getting caught in the middle. "Dennis and Christopher," he mused, recalling Madame Li's words. "Those could be English names as easily as French ones." He thought things through. "If Chapdelaine received what he thought were orders to come here as a missionary, it would explain his haste but also his enthusiasm. And how he knew where to go."

Wu nodded. "Foreigners are not allowed to venture inland without express permission," he stated. "And right now, that would not be granted to any missionary. So if he means to leave Hong Kong, he would have to do so illicitly."

"Assuming this is some sort of plot, then, they mean to smuggle him out of here," Phillipe concluded. "How would they go about that?"

His companion allowed himself a small smile. "I believe I know." Rising to his feet, he handed a few coins to the shopkeeper and made for the door. Phillipe was right behind him, Dupin still gulping down a last piece of something like radish.

"I had no idea this was here," Phillipe exclaimed, stopping to stare at the low stone wall fronting the water, and the long docks extending from it in various spots, each one festooned with old-fashioned sailing ships. "A dock beneath the docks!"

Wu nodded. "The mooring towers are for foreign craft," he said. "These are for local ships. Including junk." He gestured toward a tall, slim ship with three wide sails. "That one there, it is rigged for air travel."

Now that he'd mentioned it, Phillipe noted the vents along the sides, and the pipes running just below the railings. "You think that's our ship?" He was already trotting in that direction. "Let's find out."

Men scattered out of his path, particularly when Dupin spread his wings and rose into the air, flying just above Phillipe's head. Wu hurried after. Several sailors emerged from belowdecks as Phillipe reached the ship's gangplank, hands already going to clubs and cutlasses at their sides, but a sharp word from Wu and they all backed away, empty hands held well out from their bodies.

Hurrying onboard, Phillipe ducked down the short stairs in the back—and nearly lost his head to a club that swung at him out of the darkness. Backpedaling quickly, he knocked the weapon aside, lashing out with a fist. He received a grunt of pain in return. Someone crumpled to the deck. Then a small, round shape emerged at head height. The barrel of a gun.

A man stepped out, the pistol aimed at Phillipe's chest. He was broadly built, with auburn curls and thick sideburns. "Who the hell're you?" he demanded. Definitely British.

"Parisian Police," Phillipe replied, holding himself ready. "You're under arrest."

The man laughed—and Dupin cawed at him, then flew straight at his face. "Ah!" The stranger flailed, trying to keep the bird's sharp claws and beak from tearing his flesh—and stepped into Phillipe's fist, which laid him out flat.

Peering cautiously into the little cabin beyond, Phillipe found a third man there. This one was dressed in a black cassock, and his long face matched the image he'd been shown back in Paris. "Father Chapdelaine?"

"Oui," the man replied in French. "Who are you? What is the meaning of all this?"

"I will explain, Father," Phillipe promised, showing his credentials. "But for now, if you'd please accompany me?"

Chapdelaine nodded and let himself be led off the boat. Wu had been busy tying up the other two foreigners. "My people will collect them," he promised.

"I do not understand," Chapdelaine stated again. They were seated in a small, utilitarian café near the airship docks, which Phillipe had judged the safest place for them. "I have orders from the bishop himself!" Reaching into his cassock, he produced a document and handed it to Phillipe, who scanned it quickly. It did indeed say that the priest was to travel to Hong Kong at once, then on to someplace called Quijing and from there to Xilin.

Wu nodded once he'd also read it. "Quijing is in Yunnan Province," the local inspector explained. "Safe enough. But Xilin is in neighboring Guangxi Province. The mandarin there is notoriously anti-Catholic. Being found ministering there would be a death sentence."

"I would gladly give my life for my faith," the priest insisted. "But you say these orders are false? Why would someone do that to me?" He looked devastated at the thought.

Phillipe recalled his and Wu's earlier conjectures. "I don't think it had anything to do with you specifically," he told the distraught priest as gently as he could. "Your death would shatter relations between France and China. In no time at all, we would most likely be at war."

"And then Britain would come to your aid," Wu stated, with obvious bitterness. "A ready excuse for them to invade, as they have long wished to do."

Phillipe nodded. "We were all just pawns in this," he agreed. "But we've foiled their plans, at least for now." He clapped Chapdelaine on the shoulder as he stood. "We'll get you safely back to France, and back to your flock there."

The priest nodded. "Thank you. Thank you both."

Next Phillipe regarded his local counterpart. "Thank you, Inspector Wu," he said, bowing deeply. "You have been a tremendous help, not just to me but to my nation. I will not forget it."

Wu bowed back—and then offered his hand. "Please, call me Siong."

Phillipe smiled and shook hands with the man. "And I am Phillipe. My pleasure."

Dupin squawked. "Pleasure. Hong Kong is a pleasure."

That made Phillipe laugh, and even Wu cracked a smile. "Indeed. Fare well, wūyā."

"Wūyā," Dupin repeated. "Wūyā."

Then it was time to go.

Mervat in the Maiden's Tower

Jeff Young

The aeroflot swaying in the breeze, I considered Constantinople below me, visible between my wrinkled old toes where they jutted out from my sandals. I had never seen the city from such a height. The air was for the rich or the couriers carrying the words and will of the rich. My tasks were much more earthbound. Let those with grand purpose flit about overhead, little Mervat would rather be saving lives below.

The crossroads of the East and West was somewhat visible through the smoke from homes and businesses that rose like sooty djinn above the cedar-shrouded hills counterpointed by the upthrust minarets of the mosques. Constantinople's veins crawled with locomotives chugging their way toward the center as ships plowed their way through her arteries to port. The heart of the Ottoman Empire pulsed to the sound of crying gulls, the ringing bells of the Byzantine Churches, and the call to prayer of the muezzins. I struggled to keep my greying hair under the shawl I'd tossed over my shoulders and then pulled over my head, wondering all the while what use was I, the matron of the Hospital founded by Florence Nightengale, to the harbormaster, that he would summon me so?

The lift bag of the small airship snapped like a sail, and I jerked in the harness like a fool. My pilot was an ancient fellow, though spry enough to pedal the great fan underneath the carriage through its rotations, and also occasionally to stamp the bellows to keep the coal burner lit under the lift bag. I truly wondered at his stamina, but the lines of prayer flags hanging from the prow and his features convinced me that his Himalayan background were suited to such an elevation.

With mustaches like a walrus, yellowed by either a smoking or turmeric habit, he occasionally turned around to follow the trail of little streamers of sparks flying backward from the brazier like shooting stars; perhaps only slightly concerned they might set me alight. The scent of whale oil that kept the gears from squeaking hung about us in a haze only broken by the occasional breezes. I held my shawl over my nose lest I sneeze.

With a sigh and a wary gaze, I considered the many clouds that filled the sky. Not exactly pleasant weather, and certainly not improved by the smoke from industry. For a moment the haze parted, and to my delight, sunlight flicked across the waters of the Bosphorus like a lightning flash, vanishing just as quickly. Once again, I was drawn back to the clouds, their dark roiling undersides all too close. Something more seemed to swirl within those condensed vapors... I wondered, peering upward. The vision came over me suddenly.

Stairs ascended into darkness, each anchored by the glow of two green points of light.

I shook my head until the image no longer persisted, my heartbeat erratic, my breathing shallow. I set myself the task of finding inner calm. Breathing in one nostril and out the other, I balanced myself; so much easier than if it had happened while I attended to a patient. Visions, no matter how strange, were not to be feared. My grandmother, who raised me after my parents vanished under mysterious circumstances, had made me understand that. She'd flipped through ancient books pointing out passages about the Sibyls of ancient Greece, as well as dreams brought on during the day by the gods of many religions. I still remember fondly her introducing me to many world beliefs: Greek, Etruscan, Celtic. I remember the symbols of their resulting religions, like the bull of Mithraism and the eternal Zoroastrian flame. Now those very same volumes rest in places of honor upon my own shelves.

Pulling the shawl tighter about my shoulders to dispel the chill that settled there, I contemplated the image brought to me in the vision: darkness and green lights. What could it mean? It was hard to see this as the gift from the gods that my grandmother always insisted it was. It had been years since I'd had a vision, and the timing definitely concerned me. In consideration of my current destination, perhaps it was best to set aside these thoughts for the moment.

Today certainly held many questions. What did the harbormaster want from me? And what was that looming shape on the horizon?

Could it be the Chinese dirigible of late whispers about on the streets? Why were they not allowed to land? Stuck repeating this circular loop, they became a threatening presence whose shadows darkened the streets below, making the antlike people stop and point at the sky, unlike the silvery hulls of other trade dirigibles tied up at the farthest northern portions of the port, away from the shipping lanes.

With an unsettling jerk, the aeroflot began its ungainly descent to the roof of the harbormaster's offices. My head spun as we spiraled downward. Round and round, we dropped lower, with stomach-flipping hitches, as the pilot toggled the flaps on the side of his vehicle to vent hot air. The landing snapped my chin to my chest as the aeroflot's struts thumped down on the rooftop.

Fortunately, I didn't have to pay for the journey. I untied the re-straining belt and jumped to the roof; dust fountaining up around my sandals. Before I could turn about, the brush of air from the motive fan rushed over me, and the aeroflot was away on its next journey. A door opened ahead of me, and a figure with a cloth over their mouth gestured me forward. I was only given a few moments to shake the dust from myself before being ushered into the august presence of Erhan, the Master of Haydarpaşa Port.

Seated in a high-backed wooden chair with an antelope-hide seat, I stared into the depths of the strong tea that the harbormaster had given me, waiting until he deigned to speak. After enough time had passed to try my patience, I took a full sip of tea and then gently cleared my throat. The rustling of papers came to a halt.

Before Erhan could speak, the entire office began to vibrate in sympathy with the fans of an airship passing overhead. The teacups jumped, the painted tiles on the wall chattered, and the Damascus steel kukri hanging over Erhan's desk tipped forward. With a gesture that spoke of both repetition and frustration, he reached up and pushed the blade back onto the hanger bolts without looking. Our gazes swung toward the window with its view of the blue waters of the Bosporus. The shadow of the *Alpasian* stretched out above the buildings of Constantinople. The third ship of the Ottoman fleet had arrived. Even as it joined its sister ships, the *Alpasian* was dwarfed by the floating monstrosity that was the Chinese Khongqi Long class dirigible.

Dark eyes wide, Erhan stabbed his finger toward the Chinese ship as if he could pierce its side and save the trouble of an unwelcome visitor. "These infidels and their impatience will cost us. No one wants a war with their nation, but they insist on docking without following protocols."

Completely surprising me, the harbormaster leaned forward over the desk conspiratorially and said, "There are rumors that the Black Death has come to the Empire of the Sun, and that their navy flees to safe havens."

He paused, almost as if he wasn't certain what to say next, fingers drumming on the table. "That beast up there is running on its last fumes and their crew is starving, but I will not be responsible for their bringing the plague to my city." Realizing how far he had leaned toward me; he sat back into his carved wooden chair and straightened his tunic.

Another stab of his finger; this time in my direction, made me flinch. "This is your part in things. As the head of the hospital, we will need you to assess the state of the Chinese crew. To aid in this, a temporary docking rig is being assembled and will be towed out to the Kýz Kulesi. What is it that the tourists call it?"

"It's known as the Maiden's Tower, sir. Constructed by the Byzantine Emperor Comnenus. The legends say he sequestered his daughter there after an oracle prophesied that she would die of a venomous snakebite on her eighteenth birthday. Unfortunately, a snake crawled into a basket of fruit brought in for the birthday celebration and…" I trailed off noticing the raised eyebrows of my host. "Sorry, legends and mythology are a pleasure. You were talking about a docking rig?" I prompted.

Shaking his head, Erhan continued, "Once installed and anchored to the island, it will allow the Khongqi Long ship to lower crew for review and for us to raise supplies to the ship. You will inspect the crew and make a determination of the state of their health. If necessary, you may use the Scudari Barracks for their quarantine, as your mentor, Ms. Nightengale, once did. We can also make water and food available to the crew of the ship. But no one, not a single person or creature, is coming to land from that ship until you clear them. So, Ms. Mervat, that is your task. You will, of course, need to take several nurses to aid you. I will supply you with a squad of harbor watchmen to ensure there are no military misunderstandings. Ultimately, the decision will be yours to make concerning their fate." After a hard stare, Erhan slid a pile of paperwork across his broad desk to me, took a slurp of tea, and cleared his throat, before turning back to glare at the Chinese ship floating above his port.

That, I supposed, was that. Grasping the papers and my nerves as best I could, I stood to see myself out; knees popping in protest as I struggled to my feet. I shuffled my way past the giant silver tea urn at the entrance to Erhan's office and through the door. It was a long trip as I wound my way down the stairs, occasionally stepping to one side to let a port employee with armloads of paperwork pass me by. At my age, a fall down those stairs would bring a quick end to my career. Well, I'd wanted to show them I could still do important things. If only Ms. Nightingale could see me now. Glancing back, I wondered if perhaps Erhan's exclamation was actually a sigh of relief that this was no longer his responsibility. Coming out into the main hall, I found a seat on a bench to consider the paperwork I'd acquired.

Here was a requisition for a boat. That was immediately helpful. Here was also a requisition for a squad of watchmen. Lastly, here was a writ of credit to pay for whatever was necessary. This was quite a bit. In fact, it might slow down the process of getting me to the point of diagnosing the crewmen. I closed my eyes. It was only for a moment, and it felt good. I forced them open once more, and gathering as much determination as I could muster, started for the doorway.

At the bottom of the stairs outside the office, I acquired a shadow. A very familiar familial shadow. "Whatever it is Kurnaz, the answer is, no." I planted a hand on my hip and stared at him.

"What? A cousin cannot stop to see about the welfare of their relation? Truly, do not ascribe evil where none exists."

"So, there is no reason at all you happen to be skulking about the Harbormaster's Office?"

"I resent that. I am most certainly not skulking about. I am here because you are just done with meeting one of the most important people in Constantinople, who has, no doubt, given you a task of great significance. Such an occurrence can only mean that you are in need of assistance, and Mervat, who can you trust, if you cannot trust your own blood?"

I stared at him and let the moment draw out, my scowl lingering as my mind worked at this latest surprise. The reality was that I needed someone to look after the details and let me do my work. No, I wasn't going to, there was no way I'd ever... it made... I sighed. In reality, it made perfect sense to let my busybody cousin deal with the parts that I didn't wish to, but we were going to do things my way.

"No."

"What? No consideration at all? How can you just throw away such generosity on my part?"

I had him now, but I would need to seal the deal, so I explained what was required. After I finished, he thew up his hands, huffed, and turned away from me to walk down the street. I stayed where I was. This was all part of the dance, like haggling over a rug in the marketplace.

"It's fine. I understand that it's too much for you. Maybe if I have something simpler, next time I will seek you out." He stopped in his tracks. "Look it's perfectly straightforward. You would be acting in my name to make sure that—" I started.

"It's nurses. What do I want to do with nurses? Unless…is Salome still—you know of whom I speak, the one with eyes like deep wells—" He looked back over his shoulder at me, smoothing his thinning hair across a broad forehead.

"I will choose the nurses. You will organize the watchmen. You will get the boat. You will make sure that they can set up the docking tower. That is quite a bit of responsibility. Perhaps I should find someone else…"

Kurnaz spun about, retracing his steps to lunge forward and catch at my arm, "Now, cousin, do not be hasty in your choices. I am certain you could find someone willing to deal with all of this, and you do have to admit it is quite a bit. But—and consider this carefully—who else really would be foolish enough to get involved without a hefty payment?"

I turned away, so he couldn't see my grin. I wiped it from my face as swiftly as possible. To catch Kurnaz one only had to use the right bait. Now that I had him though, I would have to play him like a fish on the line, for his interest was sure to wane over time. At the moment, the promise of authority and money would work. "Here is the writ for the boat. It's best we start there so that we know what we are walking into. Kýz Kulesi hasn't been used in years, and we're going to have to turn it into a dock *and* a medical facility. Contact me as soon as possible." I didn't need to look up to remind him of the threat overhead.

"Cousin, we didn't discuss payment…"

I shook my head at him, "You will be paid, that's all."

"Fine, then meet me at the docks in an hour," Kurnaz said confidently.

My sharp look helped him to reconsider. "No, I will see you after midday."

"Fine," his tone indicated understanding, and a little contrition.

That was perfect for me. It gave me time to pack and collect my bag of medicines and tools. Then it was across the water to the Tower.

I stepped around the dog drinking from a dip in the paving stones intentionally designed to collect water and looked up to the doorway of my hospital. Before continuing, I turned back to gaze at the cur's brindled fur. There were days when I loved living in a city that carefully looked out for its animal inhabitants, but wasn't it strange to see so many dogs and no cats? Ah well, I thought, it was as Grandmother said, "Men lead dogs where they like, and cats go where *they* like."

Smiling and shaking my head, I reached out for the railing to ascend the few steps into the building. When my hand clasped the cold metal, it sent a shock through me. The sounds of the city faded in and out. All of my senses dulled save that of my inner eye. So soon? After so long without? I swayed as a beam of sunlight breaking through the overhead haze caught my gaze and sent my perceptions elsewhere.

Over a wall, the water surged back and forth, and from the skies fell metal and flames that hissed as they struck the waves.

My heart stuttered like it had missed a beat. At my sharp intake of breath, the dog turned and looked at me. Its small whine of concern brought me back to myself. I'd slumped against the smooth wall, my cheek against the cool stone. Blinking rapidly, I pushed myself upright, rocking back onto my feet to straighten my dress and nurse's apron. I was relieved this episode had gone unnoticed by anyone from the hospital. I needed my people to trust me, especially if we might be headed into dangerous circumstances. I couldn't appear weak or incapacitated.

Even so, I trembled, my belly twisting like an agitated nest of snakes. What had I seen? An airship crashing? How could I know, and just which divine entity had I to thank for sharing such cryptic signs? Focusing on my breathing, I calmed myself with the assurance that such glimpses showed me only one *possible* future. Grandmother always said, "People were not meant to live in the future, only in the now. The now was a cart to which humans were tethered. Sometimes you rode the cart and sometimes you pulled the cart." If only I could find a way to *steer*.

Shaking my head, I pulled open the hospital door, and scents of astringents and alcohol replaced the smoke, spice, and other street aromas. Inside waited the organized chaos that I'd made my own for the better part of my career. It took only a few moments to set people to gather necessary supplies and then briefly settle at my desk to collect my thoughts.

I'd seen the island from a distance my whole life and was always too busy to make a boat trip near it; now it would become my new office. Gnawing nervously on my first knuckle, I gave in for a second to the fear that I might not be up to this challenge. I swept my grandmother's picture off the desk and into my satchel, along with the latest book I was reading. My extensive research into mythology, combined with the burden of my parents' disappearance, left me unable to commit to one religion. Lifting my eyes to heaven in a brief prayer to Allah, on Kurnaz's behalf, since he was the believer, that he was fulfilling his duties, I stepped out into the hallway. Pushing aside these thoughts, I lifted my voice to summon my nursing staff. It was time to choose the five who would brave Kýz Kulesi with me.

The boat trip was less panic-inducing than the ride through the streets to the port in our hired supply wagon. After the first near miss, I could not bear to watch our progress through streets meant for pedestrians, so I spent more time watching the aeroflots chugging their way through the sky. The shrieks of my fellow nurses only seemed to encourage the maniac munching candied dates while snapping the reins. When we finally clambered out at the port, clutching at our supplies and bags, I made a point of giving the man the sharp side of my tongue. It did not improve my demeanor, to discover that Kurnaz, being Kurnaz, had not waited. He'd taken the watchmen ahead to the island. I took a deep breath and tried to settle myself.

It soothed me some to have the well-spoken captain welcome me, and to watch his crew efficiently load our items aboard. As we pulled away from Haydarpaşa Port, I looked across the water to the Ayasofya mosque, its four great minarets, red-painted front, and gold-topped dome making it easily visible against the green hills. Then I turned to face my destination. Kýz Kulesi, the Maiden's Tower, awaited me. A part of me thrilled to be assigned to a site of such rich history. The rest of me feared I would be too stressed to appreciate it. In the distance, the Kongqi Long Chinese dirigible floated in slow circles above the Bosporus, a harsh reminder of my purpose here. A flash visible from the bow of the dirigible indicated it was responding to instructions from the port, most likely to wait until the docking rig was raised and anchored. Three smaller flashes came from the Ottoman airships. The rocking of the boats usually eased my cares, but today those were too many to calm.

Kurnaz waited at the dock to greet me as the boat pulled alongside the small rectangular island. I noticed that he'd found some cleaner clothes, and his moustaches were oiled enough that even the wind couldn't peel them from his cheeks. The wind did, however, whip his thinning hair. He flicked it out of his eyes as he reached forward to offer me a hand getting out of the boat. We both glanced up at the airships, whose drumming fans filled the air. To our left floated the barge loaded with the iron docking rig, and Kurnaz gestured toward it. "They will winch it upright and attach it to the wall so we can move things up and down, including their men. But first we must meet with them."

"This should be a peaceful setting, Kurnaz. The watchmen are here to do the work of setting up the tower, helping the nurses put together our field office, and provide for our safety if necessary. I want you to have them leave their guns behind. We mustn't provoke the Chinese. Things will be bad enough if they are carrying the plague."

"You know best, Mervat."

I tipped an eyebrow at him.

"When you are in charge, you know best."

"Fine, I would like to see the tower now," I said, turning away. This gave me a moment to consider the wall in front of me: the very wall from my second vision. It struck me that the first vision was likewise linked. The stairs I'd envisioned while in the Harbormaster's office could very well be those leading up the interior of the famed tower.

"Why the tower?" my cousin asked, anxious to get to the task at hand.

"So, I can see everything first before starting, and that is more easily done from above." That would hopefully be enough for him.

He gestured impatiently, and I followed him toward the lone building that occupied the island. Two stories tall, it was covered in white brick, with a few windows on the second floor. A red tiled roof covered the attached entrance area. On the left side rose the tower, four square stories, followed by a window-encircled cupola that was surrounded by a metal railing and surmounted by a flagpole. A navigational light stood opposite the tower on the corner of the island and a small pier accommodated incoming water traffic.

Rustling and bustling greeted me as I passed through the doors; my nurses already unpacking the supplies we'd brought with us. I frowned at the watchmen just standing along the walls inside while my nurses wrestled with the heavy crates. Kurnaz was looking from nurse to nurse, and I reached out to push him, "She's not here, you fool. Do you think that I would bring Salome along? You would get absolutely nothing done at all. I left her in charge at the hospital. In fact, speaking of getting nothing done, why are your men standing around like that? Get them to help the nurses or this will take forever." I rolled my eyes at him and scowled, "But first, get me the keys to the tower."

Shaking his head in amusement, Kurnaz began to loudly direct the guardsmen to and fro. One of them sheepishly approached me and offered the key before returning to the fray. I surveyed the activity for a moment, tables and cots being unfolded, supplies being unboxed and organized. Satisfied that things were happening as they should, I turned to the doorway in the far wall. With my suspicions raised by the vision, I had to be the first to see what mysteries the tower might hold.

The click of the key echoed, and the draft of warm air that rolled down the steps made me hesitate. I had expected it to be cold. Diffused light reached down from above, but barely touched the darkness. I considered returning for a lamp, but the tower was only four stories tall. Surely, I could manage that.

On my first step, the stair creaked. My frown returned. If the steps were not safe, perhaps we should lock the tower to keep out the curious. As I climbed, the noise from the ground floor faded, then ceased. In fact, by the time I reached the turn that took me to the next floor, it was quiet enough that I heard the door snick shut below. Who was playing merry tricks now? With no light to see things below, I could only continue onward and hope there was a lantern to be found when I reached the rounded top floor. My outstretched hand caught the edge of a sill, and I pulled myself close to one of the archer-slit windows I'd seen from outside. It was so caked with dust that no light came through. Step by step, I proceeded upward. Halfway around, something brushed against the outside of my leg through my skirt. I stifled a scream with some difficulty. Hand over my mouth, I breathed heavily as yet another body wove about my ankles. Cats. A multitude of cats passed me, brushing against my legs. When I looked upward, all

I could see was a sea of green almond-shaped eyes staring at me out of the darkness — my vision manifested.

The little devils were everywhere. One stared at me out of the darkness from the sill I had just explored. I was determined that these felines were not going to stop me from reaching the top of the tower. I pushed myself forward. It was like wading through a warm and furry stream. The current of cats pushed against me in passing, but I hooked my arm under the railing to draw myself upward. One moment they were about my legs and the next they were up to my hips, then I was pulling myself hand over hand, gripping the railing, across their backs: my shoes no longer in contact with the stairs. Eyes zoomed at me out of the darkness, passing by in blurs. The muscles in my arms began to burn. The turn ahead indicated that I'd come all the way around the third floor. I still had four more flights of stairs ahead of me.

Amazed that none of the cats had scratched or nipped at me, I continued. I found myself stopping every few breaths to rest. The cats now slithered under my arms and across my back; fur brushing against my cheeks. Still, I pulled myself along, on and on. The first one that clambered across my head made me shriek, and at that moment, I began to wonder if it was possible to drown in cats. I hung there, so close to the final set of stairs, as if flung overboard and struggling to keep my head above waves of fur. When I felt the first of my fingers letting go, I realized that something had changed, the tide of cats receded. My feet once again touched the stairs. A little while longer and I could stand. Turning about, I considered the area below me, the entirety of the lower portion of the tower now writhed, a sea of fur punctuated by green-flashing eyes.

I caught my breath and pushed my protesting leg muscles onward; my hands numb from clutching so hard. *Fine, no way down. Well, my goal was upward, anyway.* I climbed until I could see the evening sunlight filtering through the glass windows. Back hurting, snorting as if I had run the entire way, I popped my head above the level of the floor. I was surprised to find yet another set of green eyes staring at me.

A woman was stretched out upon a divan in the center of the round room. Her long black plaited hair fell in waves above a round golden necklace embossed with images of birds and beasts. She was such a surprise that I could only stare. The stranger's white chiton was cut in a style I only recognized from books. I tore my eyes away to glance around the room. Papyrus scrolls were stacked everywhere around the walls. Black pairs of gold-chased statuary cats stood guardian beside every entrance. A single brass telescope was propped in front of an open door. A bed of rushes lay against one wall. Pushing herself up to a seated position, the occupant of the room put her hands on the edge of the divan and stared at me. Only then did I realize that the woman's shadow cast by the setting sun did not match her profile but was in the shape of the head of a feline. I almost fell down the stairs. The clues were there from all of the mythology that I had studied, but how had a goddess of ancient Egypt come here to the Maiden's Tower? A light suddenly bloomed in my mind: why was she sending me visions?

The cat goddess's voice did not pass her lips. Instead, it rose from the stairwell below, a conglomeration of sounds from her hundreds of feline followers. The flow of fur on fur, claw on stone, gentle purrs, and all of the sounds that cats make. Together they blended. Slowly, recognizable words met my ears, "Well, aren't you determined."

"I am in need, oh Bast."

"There's a name that recent centuries have found little use for. You have my attention. Do approach. I can't have you skulking at the floor like a rodent."

Perhaps years of visions had made me more likely to believe in the impossible, I thought as I ascended. Once there, I leaned against the wall at the top of the stairs. *After all, I am conversing with a goddess. I haven't completely lost my mind, have I?* Before I could stop myself, I asked, "Why are you here of all places, Bast?"

"Come now, cats love heights, libraries, stories, and such. When I was chased out of Egypt all those years ago, I needed someplace new. Here was a lovely spot to retire to, after the burning of the library."

"Burning of—wait... Alexandria?"

"A truly fateful day. I called that magical place home until the flames came; a wonderful place to retire when my name stopped coming to the minds of the people. Like the many tomes of wisdom, my faith in men became ashes that day. Only after long consideration have I come to realize that not all are torch-bearing fools."

My eyes widened and my breath caught in my throat. The gods had left their lands when their people had stopped their worship. Were there other gods out there right now?

Bast purred loudly and her gaze caught mine. I found myself unable to look away. "You said that you have need?"

I needed the island, Bast's adopted home, but how could I ask that of this forgotten god? How could I ask Bast to share her haven? Finally, it all became clear. She was the source of the visions, and even if she had never set foot in Constantinople, she was still a divine influence that looked after people. Even if they were ignorant of her presence, they were a potential source of worship. She must have waited all these years until she divined that the time was right for her to intervene. A plan came to me. Since I was in the presence of a living goddess, it was difficult to say if it was truly my creation or divinely inspired. A goddess would help the people she perceived as hers; I could ask this. As I spoke, the green light of Bast's eyes began to glow.

When I came down from the tower, I found Kurnaz waiting for me. "Where have you been? Things have come to a boil. The Chinese sent a delegation. They used a cargo winch from their ship to drop down three men." With that, he caught my hand and drew me out past the examination areas my nurses had arranged. Kurnaz stood for a moment in the doorway. Ahead of him a group of guardsmen stood in a line, their black and red uniforms topped with red fezzes. Their rifles rested at their sides, butts on the ground. Damn, Kurnaz. Hadn't I told him there were to be no guns?

Beyond them waited three Chinese in blue uniforms; the man in the middle's trimmed with gold brocade on the sleeves and shoulders. His hat was black with a red center, and a curved cavalry sword rested at his side. This wasn't a confrontation, but obviously neither side was comfortable with the current situation. "So far, they are not shooting," Kurnaz said, as he walked by my side past the watchmen's formation.

They would both put on a bold front, which was well enough. I'd dealt with plenty of men in dire straits. Injured parties who were so convinced they would never need anesthetic could be reasoned with and brought around. These were men who were frightened, and if they were good men, they had the best interests of their crew at heart. The fans of all the airships rumbled like distant thunder. To my left, I could see the barge bearing the docking tower. It would take quite a bit of engineering to get that upright, and that wasn't going to happen until I laid the groundwork. As Kurnaz and I approached, all three of the Chinese men were staring at me.

"Gentlemen," I said holding out my open hands.

"Where is the diplomat?" hissed the one on the right, "We've been forced to wait here and then they send us you? What is this? You act completely without honor. Do you fools not realize we have men starving to death above your very heads? The sick are without comfort and aid. This is intolerable. Do not press us into taking what we need. What happens will be upon your heads."

Kurnaz's eyes flew open wide, and his hand went immediately to his dagger. At the same time the man in the middle grasped the collar of the one who'd cried out, pulling him back, shoving him behind him. He looked at me, his eyes sharp and clear.

I stepped closer and said, "I am a nurse. I am sworn to aid the sick. My nurses and I are here to offer aid and to determine if you are carrying the plague. If you are not, then we can allow your ship into the port. If your men are sick, your ship will be quarantined. Your men can be treated here in a makeshift hospital we will set up in the building right over there. Regardless, we have both food and water coming on the boat you see behind us, so no one will starve."

I took a breath and then continued, "I am the administrator of my hospital, which means that I get things done. If you would rather wait for the diplomats who will spend their time talking and arguing, you are more than welcome. The Harbormaster has sent me, so let's start accomplishing something."

For a moment nothing happened but the wind flapping through the sails, and then slowly, very slowly, the man in front of me began to smile. He bowed and introduced himself, "I am Captain Shien Li of the Khongqi Long dirigible, the *Enduring Lotus Blossom*. It is always a pleasure to encounter someone who works with purpose. Please accept my apologies for my man. Like many of my crew, he is driven to extremes by the circumstances of our voyage. We will accept your terms. You may begin your examination with us, if that is suitable."

"I am pleased to meet someone who speaks our language so well, sir."

Li gestured about and said, "This is not my first trip to your city and hopefully it will not be my last."

I returned his bow and then turned to Kurnaz. "Please see that your watchmen stand aside. I will escort the captain and his men inside the building. Once they are ready, the nurses can begin the examination. Oh, and Kurnaz, I locked the tower. The stairs are not safe. Make sure the watchmen know that no one is to go up there."

Kurnaz nodded to me and then began shouting his instructions at the others. Well, I had chosen him, and I certainly should have known what I was in for.

"As for your ship, captain, I have a proposition to ensure that there are no rats aboard carrying the plague. I can send a great many cats aboard your vessel, and they will search out the vermin."

"That is a very clever solution to the problem."

"Well, sometimes one finds help in the most unexpected places."

"Indeed, madam. Indeed. My men will look forward to setting your furred warriors to their task." Li bowed low once again.

After returning his bow, I led the way to the examination area.

Several hours later, cages of burning rat corpses fell from the Khongqi Long dirigible into the waters of the Bosporus, and I understood my second vision. The feline representations of Bast had completed their task.

The *Enduring Lotus Blossom* was tethered to a tower at Haydarpaşa Port. Leaning against the railing of the top floor of the Maiden's Tower, I watched as the guardsmen pulled the temporary iron docking tower away from the wall. It would go back onto a barge for use elsewhere. Erhan had found my request somewhat unusual but hadn't balked. After all, I had produced results. Perhaps it was my influence that made the Harbormaster agreeable or perhaps it was divine intervention. I had secured the Maiden's Tower for Bast. It seemed the least that I could do.

I felt the presence at my side of the tall Egyptian goddess. Bast regarded me kindly, and then swept a feline glance in the direction of the gulls crying as they soared above the tower. From the corner of my eye, I caught the shadow of a tail flicking back and forth on the wall behind me.

"What will you do now?" I asked.

"What I always do, watch, doze, and occasionally read."

In a cat's eye, all things belong to cats, I thought. But there was still the question that would not leave. Why had she chosen me? Perhaps I was the key that made all that occurred possible, but there seemed to be something else. The revelation, when it came, was both humbling and surprising: I was the only one who would have immediately recognized her and trusted her. Since I was a witness to her actions and abilities, I could tell the story of how she had helped to avert the crisis. I could plant the seed to revive the worship of the goddess of cats. Did I, the hospital administrator, wish to become a prophet for a once-forgotten god? I had a suspicion that there might be further visions forthcoming. Then something occurred to me: Bast was a goddess tied to her nature. If I wished to avoid such a future, then I must distract her. "You've been here observing us for so long. You could always cross the water and see the city."

"Why would I do that?"

"Well, it came to me that if you represent yourself as a cat and most people see you in such a fashion, that perhaps one of your family could have already found a new home here in Constantinople."

Bast drew back from me, but I noted a curious longing in her eyes.

"There are a great many dogs running about the city. Could it be that your brother, Anubis, is here?" I had her now, but how long could I distract a goddess? Well, we would just have to see.

Bast pursed her lips and once again the shadow tail flickered, "Isn't that a thing, a thing indeed?" Her green eyes were sharp with intent. "I don't suppose there is room on your boat?"

"Oh, certainly," I said, "We'll just make Kurnaz stay until the next trip."

Ghosts in the Infernal Machine

Ef Deal

AT FIFTEEN, DIDIER RABÔT, CADET SON OF THE DUC D'ALÈSE, WAS neither Legitimist nor Republican, and the only "Rights of Man" he cared about was his own right to exist in peace and quiet to tinker with his electrical experiments, preparing for his entrance exam to the École Polytechnique, having eschewed the traditional military service. Paris political radicals meeting upstairs from his little apartment on Boulevard du Temple arguing about the right to vote, the right to dissent, or the right to be heard (*and how could their declamations not be heard throughout the quarter?*) had spent the past two weeks denying Didier the only right that mattered to him. Now the little fellow upstairs had taken up a carpentry project, hammering night and day, clanging scrap-metal pipes, cursing loudly in Italian.

In disgust, Didier set aside his wires and nails and dead frogs to head downstairs to the café at street level. Nina, the mistress of his noisy upstairs neighbor, blocked the stairway. A hideous young woman with a mutilated hand and missing eye, she nevertheless thought herself a seductive creature, the kind to which the word "scrofulous" doubly applied.

"Salut, Monsieur Rabôt."

Even her voice was slimy. Didier squirmed past her, trying to ignore her sizable bosom shoved into his face and the sour odors her unwashed body exuded.

Though the heat of the July afternoon had stifled business at the bar, flâneurs occupied the sidewalk tables, watching the games of boules on the green. *Claque!* "Hourra!" *Claque!* "Hourra!" Who would have thought little old men in berets and blue workman's coats would have enough mastery of geometry and physics to place little round balls right where they needed to go? They reminded Didier of the men upstairs, arguing who should be where in government and maneuvering their forces to position men who would do their will.

"What are you looking at?" a gruff voice demanded.

Three national guardsmen surrounded Didier. The 8th Legion of the National Guard had begun mustering for the grand defile the next day, when the King would make a great show of reviewing the troops— *all of the troops!*—along the boulevard from Place de la Bastille up to République. Pugnacious, belligerent, and cocky, they'd been harassing his neighbors all day.

"Get off the green, dirty scum." They shoved him back. "Clear out. Don't let us catch you loitering here again."

"I'm not loitering. I live here," Didier protested. "This is my neighborhood."

One of the soldiers seized him by the collar and hoisted him off the ground. "It's our neighborhood now." He threw him to the ground. "Get lost. Don't let me see you again."

Dejected, Didier took his sorry self across the Seine to the familiar student taverns in the Latin Quarter hoping to find some camaraderie among the polytechs. In the corner of the upstairs room of *Les Mômes Vont Bien,* one of the quieter taverns, his friend Jacky sat back with her bare feet propped up on a table, perusing notes and sipping beer. Their companion Yves, an older student, bent over his textbook, underscoring passages and scribbling notes in between lines.

Didier liked Jacky, but not in any romantic way. She was an odd girl, lanky, always dressed like one of the guys, cutting her hair short to avoid having it burned off or caught in machinery, tucking it up under a cap instead of a bonnet. But she was pretty much a genius at fourteen, and she enjoyed engineering sciences as much as he did. Yves, on the other hand, wasn't as clever. His academic struggle gave him a saturnine nature. Didier didn't understand how the two got along so well.

Jacky nudged a chair toward Didier with her toe. "Didi! How goes your project?"

He slumped into the seat. "Poke a dead frog and the leg kicks. Once. I don't see where it can go."

"Try potatoes." She offered him one of her frites. "They taste better than frogs and you'll get a stronger electrical output if you link them like a daisy chain."

"Or if you boil them," said Yves without lifting his head from his notes. "Five times the electrical output. Maybe more."

"To what end?"

Jacky shrugged. "Carbon arc lamp?"

"Enough potatoes can keep it going a few days," Yves agreed.

Didier snarled. "If you know that already, I won't exactly be discovering anything, will I?" He ate the fried potato slice. "I want to do something big, like a dirigible hot-airship, run with electricity."

"Don't we all?" Jacky finished her beer and called for two more. "There's no money in airships. The government won't back you, and you'll go broke trying to fund it on its own merit. I've looked into it. Even Pauly dropped the airship in favor of weapons. Governments always have enough money for weapons."

"Weapons. Governments." Didier accepted the beer with a nod of thanks. "You sound like the crazy Corsican upstairs bitching about politics. The Society of the Friends of the Society of the Rights of the Society of Man in a Society of the Society of Socialistic Republican Legitimists." He scoffed, then drank deeply.

Yves sniffed. "Tearing down the new government they rebuilt when they tore down the old government they rebuilt when they tore down the even older one."

"I think the Corsican is rebuilding it by hand." Wiping foam from his lip, Didier frowned with a sudden frightening thought. "You know, last week they were arguing about the King. Now, he's building something in his apartment, right at the outer wall, near the window overlooking the King's route for the review. You don't suppose…"

"Probably."

"Almost certain."

Didier looked from one to the other. "Well, parbleu, should I tell someone?"

"Probably."

"Almost certain."

"What if he finds out I reported him? He'll kill me. The guy's dangerous," Didier protested. "He keeps a knife in his boot and lets everyone know he'll use it. He whips his girlfriend with a flail. I can hear them screaming at each other."

"Sounds dangerous."

"I'd leave it alone."

"But the King!"

"Probably."

"Almost certain."

He thumped his mug down angrily. "A lot of help you two are."

"Oh, you want help?" Jacky grinned. "Why didn't you say so?"

The trio finished their beers and frites and strolled back to the Place de la République and Boulevard du Temple in the fading day. More and more legions of National Guard filled the boulevards radiating from République, nudging folks from sidewalk tables and eyeing pedestrians suspiciously. When the three friends finally approached the Jardin Turc, they encountered a line of guardsmen blocking the Boulevard du Temple, interrogating every passerby.

"This is good," Yves said. "We just tell them what we suspect."

Before Didier could stop him, Yves walked directly to the bully who had cuffed Didier earlier that day.

"Excuse me, sir, we—"

The guardsman shoved the butt of his musket into Yves' chest, knocking him on his butt. "Clear out."

Jacky hurried to Yves' aid while Didier stepped in front of him to protect him from the other guardsmen.

"You?" The bully raised his gun again to strike.

"Wait, please, listen!" Didier raised his arms. "We have information for your commanding officer. We think someone's going to kill the King."

The bully shoved Didier back. "I told you to clear out. If I see you again, I shoot."

"But the King—"

"The police already know." A second guardsman stepped up. "We got word earlier. It's already taken care of, kids. Now get out."

Didier pointed to his home beyond the line of soldiers. "I live at number fifty, second floor."

"Then get there!"

Yves wiped yellow dirt and dust from his clothes. "Not me," he said. "I'm off."

He turned on his heel and trotted away, eluding Jacky's grasp. The guardsmen herded Jacky and Didier off the green. The two took refuge at the street-level café of Didier's building, where they played a game of billiards in sullen silence. Then they each ordered a plate of frites and a pin of beer to take up to Didier's rooms. They huddled in the antechamber, their voices hushed in case the racket from above wouldn't cover their talk.

Jacky said, "Do you think that guy was telling the truth? The police already know?"

Didier shook his head. "There'd be police here already, given all the noise."

"What do you figure he's building?"

"I don't know." Didier paused. "It's heavy, though. It sounds like it's difficult for him to hammer, so, heavy timbers? Oak, maybe?"

"That's a lot of work just to take a shot. He already has a perfect vantage for assassination, if that's his intention."

"But with scrap metal? The other day he hauled a bunch of tubes up the steps and dropped a few. They were stamped 'rebut.' I figured he was building a cheap pipe organ."

They both flinched at his words, "jeu d'orgue," realizing the alternate use of the phrase.

"Mon Dieu, an organ canon." Jacky gulped. "An infernal machine. If those tubes were rifle barrels, he could take out the King and his entire family, his entire entourage."

"But the place is crawling with guardsmen," Didier said. "How could he hope to get away with it?"

"Maybe he doesn't plan to get away. Martyr to the cause."

Didier leaned his head against the windowsill to get some air. Movement in the breeze caught his eye and he twisted around, then reached out the window to catch hold of a rope that rested along the wall half a meter from his window, dangling down to a lower roof.

Jacky joined him and peered up. "So he does plan to get away. Now we know."

Didier released the rope with a sigh.

Jacky sat beside him. "We can't electrify rope. So, what else?"

Didier reached for another frite but halted with it halfway to his mouth. "We could potato it." He grabbed a handful of the greasy slices and pressed them into the rope as far up and down as he could reach. "Maybe he'll slip and break his leg or something."

"Maybe. It doesn't save the King."

Didier held out a handful of the thick slices. "But we *can* electrify some wires we weave through the rope and hook it up to some potatoes."

"Still doesn't save the King." Jacky got up. "But it does help the cause. I'll go downstairs and ask if the cook will sell me a couple of boiled potatoes. Do you think you have enough zinc and copper to electrify them?"

"I think so."

"Good. Keep thinking."

When she left, Didier headed into his kitchen, which doubled as his laboratory, to get suitable wires for the rope. He hadn't thought of linking the potatoes to increase the current, but even so, at best it would give a quick shock before it frittered out. There had to be something more they could do to thwart a cannon.

The Corsican upstairs began fighting with Nina again; their caterwauling blasted at him through his back window. Cursing, pleading, roaring, insulting. Then Didier caught a threat that stuck with him: *I'm loading the chambers and you keep bitching at me! Do you know what would happen if I made a mistake with all this powder and shot?*

As Didier went to the window to listen more closely, a plan began to formulate.

"…if I make a mistake…"

While the two bickered in the back room upstairs, Didier hastily wove wire into the rope outside the antechamber and wrapped more short wires around a couple of pennies, anticipating Jacky's potatoes. She returned with twelve boiled potatoes, and the two began slicing and linking them with zinc and copper. As they worked, Didier told her about the argument he'd overheard.

"What do you think? How do we get him to make a mistake?"

Jacky didn't answer right away, but she chewed at the inside of her cheek. Didier had learned that meant she was lost in thought. He wished he had her ability to formulate designs in her head and see them as clearly as if she had drawn them on paper. No wonder she'd been accepted to the Polytechnique when she was barely thirteen.

"I'll ask the cook for funnels." she asked. "Got any tubing?"

Didier shook his head. "Just wire."

"All right." Jacky wiped her hands clean. "Start coiling around something thin, like a pencil. I'll be back."

"How long?"

"Five minutes?"

Didier snickered. Jacky caught on, and she laughed.

"Just keep coiling, as much as you can. We have to reach the upstairs shutters. Let's hope they keep fighting."

She put on her cap and slipped out the door, leaving Didier to ponder what Jacky had dreamed up. He had coiled almost the entire ten-meter spool of zinc wire before she returned, two tin funnels in hand and a dark scowl on her face.

"What's wrong?"

She waved his question away, but when she took off her cap, she sported a swollen right eye.

"What the devil?"

She ignored him, setting the funnels down to examine the coil. "This looks good."

"Jacky—"

"All right. Call it a spiteful act of vengeance. I told that guard he was a bully and probably a coward, so he punched me." She flashed a wicked grin, then winced. "When I went down, they all realized he'd hit a girl, and his fellows hauled him away." She made a little flourish. "Now, a very important element of our little design. Do you keep a sheath with you?"

Didier gasped, staring at her in shock. "Wh—A sheath?" He gulped. "Why would we need—"

He tried not to envision himself donning one in her presence. He'd never thought of her romantically; they were friends. Not that she wasn't attractive in a non-alluring way. In fact, by candlelight, she had a comfortable beauty he found fascinating. But he would never... In fact, he *had* never...

Then he caught the mischief in her dancing eyes. With a giggle, Jacky tweaked his nose.

"Sorry. I'm teasing you. I know full well you're a gentleman."

She took an etui from her vest pocket and opened it to reveal a number of small instruments along with a folded linen handkerchief from which she carefully withdrew a sausage casing, slightly stretched.

Didier slapped his brow. "Now I've seen everything."

"You really should keep one or two in a pocket somewhere, Didi. A guy like you, smart, good-looking. You never know when some pretty coquine will take you unawares."

"Jacky!" He was glad for the dim candlelight in the room so she couldn't see his blush.

"Don't worry. I've never used it. No one wants a girl like me anyway. But my sister tells me I should always carry one, so I do."

Didier would have argued, but he didn't want to give her the wrong impression about his feelings for her. He focused instead on her purpose for the prophylactic device.

She secured one end of the sausage casing over the outlet of one funnel before threading it into the coil, stretching gently until it peeped out the other side, where she knotted it. She then blew into the funnel, easing the slowly inflating casing through the stretching coil. When she finished, she sealed her end, wrapped the two ends around the edges of the coil, and slid those into the funnels.

"A lovers' whisper tube," she declared with a wry grin. "Ironic use of a virgin's sheath, non? The compressed air in the balloon concentrates sound waves, so it will not only carry my voice, but enhance it. He'll never figure out where it's coming from."

Didier examined the contraption in amazement. "You think it will work?"

He took one funnel end and carefully moved across his apartment into the antechamber, about ten meters. He pressed the funnel to his ear, and Jacky spoke softly into the other funnel. As clearly as if she stood beside him, he heard her say, "Never doubt a Duval design."

He answered through the tube. "I don't doubt the design, but how does this help our cause?"

She summoned him back and pointed to the window. "While those two upstairs are screaming at each other, we're going to slide this up the outside wall and fix it behind the shutter with spirit gum." Her eyes narrowed. "I assume you have spirit gum?"

"Of course." He riffled through a drawer in his cupboard, grumbling, "Just because I don't keep a sheath in my pocket…"

The next phase of Jacky's plan proved trickier than the science.

"You stand on the windowsill, and balance yourself with your hands inside the window." Jacky removed her boots. "I'll take care of the rest."

Didier complied, then waited impatiently. "What's taking so long?"

"I have to wash my feet," she answered. "And—other things."

Other things?? Girls.

But Didier quickly appreciated Jacky's concerns when she slipped out the window in nothing but her chemise to facilitate wrapping herself around him, then climbed up his body to stand on his shoulders. The maneuver required utter silence on their part, but the Corsican had closed his blinds to conceal his construction efforts from view, so the pair had some leeway to move about.

Once Jacky secured the mouth of one funnel to the back of the shutter close to the upper window, they found retreat more challenging. Jacky flexed her knees while Didier counter-balanced, straining to remain against the wall to keep from dumping Jacky to the café canopy below. She lowered herself to sit atop his head before sliding down the front of him. She pulled him inside after her and the two tumbled to the floor, gasping and suppressing their laughter.

"What now?" Didier asked. "I still don't see what we're using this for."

She whispered in his ear with a soft, very un-Jacky voice. "Pack the barrels. Tighter. Oh, so tight. Did you use enough powder? No, you need more powder. How much shot did you pour? Not enough. Your aim is off. Higher, lower, get the charcoal ready, more powder, more shot, pack them, pack them."

He recognized the end goal of her plot. "If he tamps the barrels too firmly, they'll backfire on him, or redirect his aim."

She grinned, her swollen black-butter eye gleaming in the candle-light. "I hope I can get him to blow his own head off."

From upstairs, a slammed door and tromping down the steps signaled the lovers' quarrel had ended and the Corsican was alone. A few moments later, the sound of a file on wood indicated he was back at his project.

"Now," Jacky said, "get undressed and go to bed. You have to be in your nightshirt only, in case the guy comes knocking."

With misgivings, Didier tucked himself into the antechamber to strip down and returned to his bedroom holding his clothing in front of him like a shield.

Jacky, in the meantime, fluffed out her hair and curled it with some grease from the leftover frites.

"What are you doing?"

She preened. "Just because I get into fights, you think I don't keep a toilette?"

Didier found it difficult to keep his eyes turned aside. He swallowed the lump in his throat and headed to his bed.

"I'll wake you when I'm ready," Jacky said. "We have to wait until he quiets." She snuggled down to curl on the floor beneath the window.

Didier tossed her one of his pillows, blew out the candle, then tucked himself under a sheet, but he couldn't sleep. The King's life was likely in their hands, and he still didn't know what Jacky's plan was.

Jacky. Stripped and sleeping in his bedroom. All the talk of sheaths and Didier's good looks, and there was Jacky—Jacqueline Duval, that is—right there in his room. How was he supposed to sleep when all he could see was her golden curls bouncing in the glow of the candle and her breasts bouncing beneath her chemise? Didier moaned quietly and pressed his pillow over his head, trying to ignore his body's natural response.

The King. The King. Close your eyes and think of the King...

He tossed and flipped over and kicked off his sheet, then quickly covered himself again. Meanwhile, Jacky's breathing came in quiet, even sounds for the next few hours, though the Corsican's tapping, filing, and occasionally spilled shot resounded through Didier's room like thunder into the deepest hours of the night.

Once the noise stopped, Jacky sat bolt upright.

"Psst! Didi!"

"I'm awake," he whispered.

"Got a blanket? I need to hide."

She threw her pillow back to him and snatched the blanket he tossed her way.

"You stay in bed," she told him. "If he knocks, make him wait, like you're asleep."

Didier grumbled. "You think anyone could sleep through all that?"

Jacky didn't answer. In the pitch dark of the unlit apartment, he couldn't even see what she was doing, and he heard no sound from her. Footsteps thumped his ceiling, then quieted. He measured the dead silence of the night in drops of sweat beading on his brow and dripping down his neck. Again, the footsteps, passing from the middle room to the window, pausing, then slowly retreating. Twenty minutes. The ritual repeated. Another half hour, another trip to the window. Finally, after two more passes, a curse in Italian.

"Show yourself, puttana!"

Jacky scuttled to the antechamber, gave a loud, mocking laugh out the back window, then crawled into the kitchen.

The Corsican ran down the stairs to bang on Didier's door. "Open up, you little scum! I know she's in there."

Didier waited before lighting his candle and going to the door. "Who is it? What do you want at this hour?"

The Corsican pounded furiously. "Give her to me, Rabôt! You send that little slut out here!"

"Go away. There's no one here but me." Didier thumped the door.

Shouts from the other rooms joined his, and the Corsican answered them with equal rage. Suddenly, Nina's voice cut through the clamor, and the man turned his anger on her. Wherever she'd been holed up from him, she was now drunk enough to fight back until the concierge appeared, in nightshirt and cap, to separate them. Nina left, screaming curses.

"I thought it was a thief, but no! Rabôt's got a girl in his room," the Corsican cried.

"That is a slanderous lie." Didier finally unlocked his door and cracked it open. "This crazy man, he hammers all day, and now he wakes me up at night? With lies?"

Before the concierge could answer, the Corsican kicked the door wider and stormed into the apartment, casting about wildly. "I heard a woman. Where is she?"

Didier trusted Jacky to have hidden herself sufficiently. He ushered the concierge in and let him tour the apartment.

"I told you, there's no one else here. I was asleep. This man —"

The Corsican went to the window. Didier held his breath, but the man found nothing he was looking for. He came back to shove his face up into Didier's.

"You've made a *mistake*," Didier said calmly. "You've made a terrible *mistake*."

The Corsican, swarthy as he was, visibly blanched at the word. He stalked away.

"I apologize, Monsieur Rabôt." The concierge mopped his brow with his nightcap. "All the goings-on. Guardsmen arrested. King's review tomorrow. Imagine, accusing you, a fine young man."

Didier yawned widely for show. "It's not your fault. Just let me go back to sleep."

"Of course, of course. Until tomorrow."

Once Didier closed the door, he waited until the building was silent again before going back to his bed. The only sound was the Corsican pacing above.

"All safe?" Didier called, sotto voce.

Giggling quietly, Jacky crawled from the kitchen to sit back against the bed. "All he heard was a phantom voice of a woman telling him he had it all wrong and mocking him." She laughed, but her voice broke. "But is it enough? I don't know, Didi." She sighed and rubbed her temples. "If only the guardsmen had listened to us."

Didier climbed out of bed to sit beside her on the floor. "I don't know what more we can do. Maybe the police have something planned and we just haven't heard about it. Or maybe the smarter guard said something to an officer, and they'll be on alert tomorrow."

"What if we try to tell the King directly when he approaches?"

"With all those legions? They'd shoot us."

"Probably."

He snickered. "Almost certain." His heart warmed when the mischievous smile returned to her face.

Notre Dame's bourdon sounded in the distance. The two bowed their heads in exhaustion.

"Zut. Matins." Jacky yawned. "I better get out of here. Find somewhere to get some sleep. You should, too."

Didier stood and helped her to her feet. "Shouldn't we wait?"

She wagged her head. "When that thing goes off, we don't want to be anywhere near here. Certainly not in the Corsican's thoughts when he blows himself up or tries to get down that rope."

Didier understood the logic, but he still caught her back by the hand when she headed for the door. "Wait!"

She searched his face. "What?"

He really wanted to kiss her, or at least tell her how beautiful she looked, and how dizzying the night by her side had been, so full of revelations.

Instead, he cleared his throat. "Clothes?"

She glanced down at herself. "Trivialities."

She padded away to find where she'd left her clothing while Didier sat and pulled on his pants, pondering the odd fact that the wonders of science had brought him Jacky Duval barefoot in her underwear. Perhaps he should direct his attention to the science of sound for his entrance exam to see what other wonders might await.

He finished tying his cravat while Jacky tucked her greasy curls back up under her cap. Together, the two slipped away into the dawn like two ghosts.

THE SAND BOAT

JAMES CHAMBERS

THE STREETS OF CAIRO REVEALED THEMSELVES LIKE THE PASSAGEWAYS OF a maze with no dead-ends. Morris Garvey and Madame Marceline Marie crossed yet another market square full of vendors hawking cotton textiles, dates, dried mullet, fresh falafel, and pottery. The aromas and voices combined with the heat of the day to create a sensory experience utterly unlike that of walking the streets of New Alexandria, Morris's home city, half a world away. He found it dizzying and exciting, even disorienting at times when he gazed down a long, narrow lane laddered with light and shadow and pockmarked by arches and doors, gateways to deeper parts of the urban labyrinth. The scent of cumin clung to his nostrils, flavoring every breath.

He lagged a few steps behind Marceline, lingering to savor the sensations of this latest market. He knew enough Arabic to understand the barking salesmen, but too little of its Egyptian dialect to follow the rapid-fire conversations of passersby and customers haggling at each stall. Marceline, who'd visited Cairo many times before, strode purposefully through the throngs of market-goers, her gait impatient. She gestured at Morris to keep up.

Morris jogged to her side then matched her step. "Marceline, why such a hurry? We find ourselves with an unexpected free day to explore the city, and you're dragging me through it as if we're on the run."

"Oui, Morris, we are on the run because I have explored these streets many times and have no wish to wander them in this heat," Marceline said. "I have arranged a surprise for you, and you are on the verge of ruining it."

"I am? How am I supposed to know that if it's a surprise?"

Marceline hurried along a street of housefronts, and Morris kept pace. They walked several yards then took another turn, then two more, then entered a small plaza, the center of a wheel with the mouths of avenues and alleys for its spokes. Shaded by close-built buildings of dried-mud bricks, limestone, and sandstone, the square offered a cool, quiet respite. Marceline took Morris by one arm and pointed down an avenue wider than the rest. At its far end a blue ribbon shimmered in the sunlight.

"See that, mon chéri? That is the Nile." Marceline pulled a pocket watch from the folds of her turquoise dress, a custom-tailored version of the traditional kalasiris, topped with a royal blue silk shawl, glanced at the time, and frowned. "You frustrating man! If we do not reach the river in time, we will miss our riverboat to Giza, and if we miss our riverboat we will miss our caravan to the Great Pyramids, and if we do not see the Great Pyramids while you are in Egypt, I will have to suffer your complaints the whole way back to New Alexandria when you conclude your business here. Comprenez-vous? Now stop dawdling and let me surprise you."

"Why, Marcy, that's the most selfish thoughtful thing anyone's ever done for me. Of course, we must not miss the boat. Let's step lively."

Morris took the lead now, rushing down the avenue with the shimmer of the great river in his sights, Marceline pacing behind him—until both of them came to a sudden, stumbling halt, bumping into one another. Three men in black gallibayas and turbans flowed out of shadowy doorways and blocked their path. The men alone did not deter their progress so much as the gleaming khopeshes brandished in their hands. The tallest, their apparent leader, shouted an order for them to halt, which Morris understood, followed by a string of challenging words he did not. A loose scarf encircled each man's neck, one black, another gray, and, for their leader, calico, all tugged up to cover the lower half of their faces. The leader gestured with his khopesh and repeated his demands.

"Are they robbing us?" Morris asked Marceline.

"They want us to go with them. I think they're abducting us," Marceline said before she put her hands on her hips and yammered back at the men in angry Arabic. The trio exchanged puzzled glances.

"Did you tell them we have a riverboat to catch?" Morris said.

"I asked them how dare they interfere with a French national on a duly appointed diplomatic mission, and Morris Garvey, the world's most famous inventor of steam technology here at the invitation of the mayor of Cairo himself. I thought that might be more persuasive than complaining about missing our riverboat."

The leader grumbled a reply to Marceline then snapped orders to his men. One seized Morris at the point of his khopesh, while the other grabbed Marceline by the arm.

"I take it they weren't persuaded," Morris said.

"Merci beaucoup, Morris. It seems, unfortunately, I inadvertently confirmed that we are the people they were instructed to capture," said Marceline.

Closer to the men, Morris observed that each wore a faience ring on the fourth finger of their right hand. Depicting a reclining cat coiled around each man's digit, they almost glowed in the morning sun.

"Perhaps we erred in going out unarmed," Morris said.

"Tut! We have the protection of the mayor. This is a most serious breach of international decorum," said Marceline.

"Do Egyptian swordsmen concern themselves with international decorum?" Morris said.

The tall man hollered and pointed. Clear enough to Morris that he wanted them to stop talking and walk. Marceline understood the message too. They strode along the avenue until their kidnappers directed them down a narrow, winding side way that terminated in an undeniably ominous darkness, a stain on the brightness of the city. Morris glanced once more at the distant Nile and sighed as it fell out of sight. They trod the uneven stone path, each step nearer the impenetrable void, bringing Morris closer to the conviction that he and Marceline might never return from this trip. He clung to the hope that if the men had merely wanted them dead, they would've slain them in the street and had done with it, but that provided little comfort.

As the darkness ahead coalesced into the alcove of a sunken doorway, a call like a falcon's cry sounded then reverberated along the alleyway. Responses came from too many directions for Morris to count and filled the air with shrill vocalizations. The black-garbed men shifted into fighting stances, khopeshes high. They diverted their gazes to the nearby roofs and doorways. Morris read fear in their rugged eyes.

The falcon cries came again, a shrieking chorus, before six men emerged from the nooks and shadows of the alley before and behind them, surrounding Morris, Marceline, and their abductors. Each one wore a silver-white gallibaya and matching turban. Each wielded a sharp-edged, steel crook in one hand, and a leather flail in the other. Then the six men converged on them.

Marceline slapped the face of her captor and yanked herself free. "Head down, Morris. There's going to be a tussle, I'm afraid."

Morris elbowed his guard, who released his grip on his arm, more concerned with the two armed men closing on him. He seized Marceline and pulled her into a doorway. Black cotton and silver-white cloth fluttered in streaks of motion, tattered sails whipped by whirling storm winds of violence. Steel rang and leather strips whip-cracked. Flickers of silver followed. Then claret sprays of blood. The men in black fought with vicious determination, khopehses flashing and whirling, even felling one of the men in silver and white, but, out-numbered, the three soon succumbed and fell dead on the ground in bloody pools.

Two of the victors tended to their fallen comrade. The other three approached Morris and Marceline. Blood dripped from their crooks and flails. They made eye contact for several seconds, as if seeking the answer to an unspoken question, then one gave out a falcon cry. Two departed down an adjoining alley, carrying away their casualty. The others stepped back, allowing a man, emerging from a nearby doorway, to join them.

Garbed in a blend of Egyptian and European styles, in his late twenties, perhaps, around the same age as Morris and Marceline, tall, lanky, and muscular, he held a walking stick with a handle carved into a crook. A thick, black beard covered his jaw. He tipped his Homburg, exposing a head of equally dense dark hair.

"Are you hurt?" he asked. "I was afraid my friends might arrive too late. I only learned this morning of the plans to abduct you and barely had time to reach some of Khonshu's Protectors of the Way, but let it not be said that the Cult of Bast may operate in Cairo without attracting the interest of Amun Zaki."

"Zaki? I've heard of you, haven't I?" Morris said.

"It is possible, indeed, as I have heard of you, Mr. Garvey. We have many common interests," Amun said.

"Do you know why these men tried to abduct us?" said Marceline.

"I do, and they will try again when this trio fails to deliver you to their master. Since it seems you're both unharmed, I suggest you follow me to a safer setting where I can explain why your lives are threatened every second you spend in my country."

"It was no coincidence that you found yourselves at loose ends today," Amun said.

The implications of the statement did not sink into Morris's thoughts right away. The steam-powered watercraft that carried them upriver along the Nile preoccupied him as he studied its construction and works, noting the unique touches of Amun Zaki's design. He and Marceline sat together on a cushioned bench. Amun occupied the pilot's seat, steering. A welcome river breeze cooled them.

Morris found travel along the Nile dream-like, the great waterway larger and more quietly powerful than any other natural formation he knew. The wind lufted the sails of passing feluccas. Men rowed fishing galleys, trailing nets, while leaf-shaped scoops fitted with large rudders ferried people with the current. Amun's unique craft extruded a steam plume that trailed into the sky, into infinity for all Morris could discern the dividing line between blue water and blue heavens in the intense brightness and tranquility of the soft river haze.

"Yes. Amun Zaki," Morris said. "You lectured at the annual conference of steam engineers in Edinburgh two years ago, published in the proceedings, where I read it some months later. Your observations helped me with my own work at the time. It's a pleasure to meet you. I had hoped to do so during my time in Cairo, but Mayor Eskander told me you were far too busy with your work to make the time. I wonder, what is it that kept you so occupied?"

Amun's expression warmed around a broad smile. "Competing with you, sir, Mr. Garvey."

"How so?" asked Morris.

"I believe a steam-based modernization of our Nile shipping and transportation should come from Egyptian minds. I wanted to build something to outclass whatever you might design for the mayor and his administration. So starstruck were they all at the prospect of the great Morris Garvey, inventor of the steam-powered chimney sweep, pioneer of miniaturized steam power, lending his genius to our humble nation, they dismissed me out of hand once you accepted their invitation. I mean no offense, effendi." Amun offered Morris a shallow bow. "They only wish for modern nations to see Egypt as an equal heading into the future, not merely an echo if its ancient glories. I want to prove we can be both and attain those glories once more."

"I see," Morris said.

He eyed the three Protectors of the Way, standing watch, one at the bow of Amun's boat, the other two at the stern. Like their would-be abductors, these men also wore jewelry identifying their dedication to divinity, crescent moon amulets of pure silver on silver chains around their necks to honor Khonshu, god of the moon, ruler of night, protector of travelers, and watchman of the night roads. They had kept them tucked away during combat but revealed them like badges once the boat set off from the riverbank. The silver gleamed in the sunlight. Now and then, the men chirped or shrilled to each other, using a complex code of mimicked falcon calls to communicate in honor of their god's depiction as a man with the head of a falcon. Only after sunset, Amun had explained, would they speak, a vow taken to honor their god.

"So, Mr. Zaki, if I understand correctly, you hope to show me up, this Cult of Bast wanted to abduct me and Madame Marie, and still others wish us both dead. Why did you not let them succeed? Wouldn't it have improved your chances of swaying Mayor Eskander to support your homegrown approach?" Morris said.

"Perhaps. But it would've been a crime to allow those villains to rob the world of your genius, Mr. Garvey. We inventors must stick together at times, don't you agree? I have no interest in your demise. We are rivals, not enemies. And if the Cult had captured you, I'm afraid the outcome would've been far more dire than a bruise to my cultural pride. Imagine the blemish to my country should two dignitaries of your renown vanish here. I do not share Bast's adherents' vision for Egypt's future."

"What did they want with us?"

"My informants told me they intended to transport you north to the city of Bubastis, where their cult thrives, to sacrifice you to their goddess. Like cats stalk mice to drop at their master's feet, the cult brings men to Bast."

"Allez! Enough chit-chat." Marceline squinted against the river brightness but also scrutinized their rescuer. "How do we know we have not leapt from the frying pan into the fire? Where are you taking us?"

"Giza," Amun answered. "You intended to go there today, didn't you?"

"Oh! How do you know that?" Marceline asked.

"I have informers all around Cairo. People who've known me since I was a mischievous boy will share with me information they would not breathe to any other soul because they know I always have Egypt and her people's best interests at heart."

"Mon Dieu! You sound like a child. Shall I put my trust in a child?" Marceline slumped against the side of the boat, crossed her arms, and sighed. "This is not the day I imagined for us, Morris."

"Mr. Zaki, tell me what you meant when you said Madame Marie and I did not find ourselves at loose ends today by coincidence. Until last evening, I looked forward to a full day of scouting along the Nile with Mayor Eskander, studying river currents, seeking serviceable port locations, then meetings with a list of city officials longer than my arm. All until… well, if you're so well informed, tell us why we had the day to ourselves."

Amun throttled the engine, slowing the boat as ahead of it appeared a line of docks and piers, so dense and busy that Morris assumed they now neared Giza.

"Your plans were cancelled because the mayor's wife fell ill with fever. Her doctors say it's a fever of the river, the kind transmitted by mosquitos. She is grievously ill and not expected to recover soon, if at all. Of course, the mayor cancelled the day's activities to sit at her side."

The steam motor thrummed and clanked as Amun slid their boat into a lane approaching the city. In the distance beyond the riverbanks, the dark points of pyramids roved into sight, prodding the horizon, and set Morris's heart racing. He listened to Amun, but the ancient structures growing larger as they neared the river port fascinated him.

"What few know, including Mayor Eskander, is that it was no insect that infected her, but a cat. One bred especially for the purpose and brought to Cairo from Bubastis a week ago," Amun said, as he angled the boat toward a dock. "There's no chance she will recover. The disease of the cat's scratch is fatal. The best one can hope is that she feels little pain and her death fails to achieve the goals of the Cult of Bast. We have thwarted their plans so far, but they will certainly try again."

At the Giza riverport, fishermen unloaded their catch. Ferry passengers disembarked or lined up to begin their trip. A sprawling market bustled with people as men sold still-wriggling mullet from the river while others hawked new nets and tackle to fishers returning to the water. The sun beat down over all of it, a hammer not pounding but resting its hot weight on Morris's skull. He fancied he could almost smell his hair burning. Marceline pulled her shawl up around her head to shade her face. Commenting on Morris's evident discomfort with his eyes squinted to mere slits, Amun led him to a stall and helped him purchase a wide-brimmed hat, which provided immediate relief.

Behind them a small crowd gathered near Amun's boat and admired its brass and steel works in wonder. A few of the gawkers turned their attention to Amun, Morris, and Marceline. They seemed to recognize Amun, but they looked upon the Protectors of the Way with fear. In the crowded market, no one came within arm's reach of them. Foot traffic streamed around them like the river around a stone.

"It's rare to see the Protectors in daylight, so they know that means trouble," Amun said. "Since the mayor announced his plans to modernize our river traffic my modest steamboat has become a cause celebré and myself with it. If only notoriety could also fund construction of a ferry to show them all what steam can do for us."

"Oui, very noble of you, Mr. Zaki," Marceline said. "Now that we're in Giza, though, will you explain why you brought us here?"

"I want you to meet a man who needs your help and who can help you," Amun said. "He awaits us at a place within the shadow of Khufu's pyramid. So, you see, I've hardly altered your plans at all, Madame Marie. You will still visit the Great Pyramids today."

"Who is this man? How can we help him?" Morris asked.

"His name is Lateef. The rest is best explained by him, but he is a long-cherished family friend who shares my hopes for Egypt's future," Amun said. "Now, please, follow the Protectors of the Way. I have arranged our transportation, and they will guide us for our safety."

"No," Marceline said. "We don't know you or Lateef. These men you call our protectors demonstrated their ability to shed blood very well this morning."

"Blood they shed in your defense," Amun said.

"Oui, but for all we know, they defended us only to help you win us away for a more awful purpose. We must return to Cairo and seek help from the French embassy and the mayor," said Marceline. "If our lives remain at risk so long as we remain in Egypt, we must cut short our visit. Morris, do you agree?"

Morris gazed at the pyramids jutting into the blue sky. He studied the crowd, pulsing with vitality, its life sustained by the Nile. He glanced at Amun's steamboat bobbing at the dock. Visions of New Alexandria stirred in his thoughts. The streets of his youth, full of crime and filth, neglected by the apathetic and the wealthy who occupied tall, clean homes on tidy avenues watched over by sanitation and police services absent from the city's other quarters. How much things had changed in the years of his growth as his city turned away from past squalor to bright new possibilities, a future he helped design. He imagined the Nile dotted with steamships, Cairo and Giza raised up on steam technology, its people stepping from their ancient past into the new century—and in the contrast he perceived something overlooked. A thriving people, yes, but a people overworked and ragged from their labors in the sun. A people trapped in a kind of poverty masked by the river's bounty, which offered them sustenance but nothing more. No foothold to climb the steps of the modernizing world, to advance from history into what the world might bring next.

"To attain those glories once more," Morris said.

"What did you say? Do you agree?" asked Marceline.

"No, Marcy, I don't," Morris said. "Everything you say makes perfect sense. Logical, cautious sense. It's exactly what anyone in our situation should do. Only, Mr. Zaki and I have more in common, I think, than our interest in steam technology. Mr. Zaki wants to give his people a future of light and progress. Marcy, have you not remarked more than once how my inventions have done the same for New Alexandria? Mr. Zaki and I are kindred spirits. I don't know how I can deny his request for help no matter what the nature of his dilemma turns out to be. We inventors must stick together. We must be stronger than those who would burden the future with the yoke of the past."

Amun offered Morris a long bow. "You honor me, sir, Mr. Garvey."

"Bluster and idealism don't suit you, Morris. If you want to visit the Great Pyramids that badly, just say so. It won't be the first time we've risked our lives for a lark." Marceline tightened her shawl around her head then stamped toward the waiting Protectors. "Lead on, you funny birdmen. I suppose, if we hang around long enough, I'll get to hear your real voices."

Morris and Amun, afraid to squander Marceline's acquiescence, dashed after her and the Protectors. The group made an unsettling sight as it traversed the city. Rarely did such a combination of luminaries walk the streets of Giza. Tourists for the Pyramids joined caravans at the riverport and rode on camel back or in wagons on roads outside the city, their presence known but unnoticed. Only archeologists and historians ventured into the city proper to purchase supplies or hire workers, but they never stayed long, living in tents and shelters at their dig sites and research locations. All this Amun shared as they walked.

After a trek deep into the city's heart, the Protectors brought them to a squat limestone building with wooden carriage doors. Amun produced a ring of keys for the many locks securing them then opened each one with a clank. He pulled the doors wide and revealed a remarkable vehicle of wood, brass, steel, and glass.

"Our means of conveyance," he said, proudly.

"It's marvelous," said Morris.

A canoe-like body formed the core of the machine, built of steel and bronze, but finished with wooden seats and cotton cushions. It sat mounted atop a chassis of more bronze and steel, fitted with crawling treads of rubber under the front half, supplemented by rear skids of hardened ceramic on brass struts. At the rear of the vehicle sat a fat boiler to power a steam engine with its parts ingeniously distributed within the framework.

"What do you call it?" Morris asked.

"My sand boat." Amun walked deeper into the shed then stopped, tensed, yanked off his Homburg, and slapped it against his leg. "No! Can one not leave a thing unattended for a moment in Giza? Is there no honor in this city?"

Morris joined him, eyeing the steam apparatus. "What's wrong?"

Amun pointed to the component that directed pressure from the boiler into the engine's working parts. Several empty fittings gaped, indicating missing pieces of machinery. "Thieves! The flea-bitten dogs have stolen the heart of my engine. How could they know to take only that part?"

"Why leave all the rest of it? They could've sold that brass for good money," Morris said.

"Sabotage. These were not mere scrap thieves. They must have known I used gold in the parts that allowed optimal distribution of pressure to the engine's branches. They took the most irreplaceable part;

one it took me nearly a year to perfect." Amun placed his hat back on his head and slumped against the sand boat. "Without my machine there is no way to reach Lateef before he assumes we are not coming and departs. Madame Marie's plan seems to be your best option now. Of course, I will see safely back to Cairo."

"I am so very disappointed," Marceline said, in a tone that expressed the exact opposite of her words.

Morris crouched and examined the gap in the engine works. He reached in, touching brass, gauging spans with his open hand, tracing lines by fingertip, then worked his way along the sand boat, following each piece of the engine to the mechanism it powered. When he stood again, he smiled.

"Don't be disappointed, Marcy," he said. "I can get this beautiful bit of engineering running again, that is, if Amun doesn't mind me tinkering with his design and repurposing a few parts. It may not be quite what it was, and I wouldn't want to cross the Saraha in it, but it'll carry us to the pyramids if not back again. So, what do you say, Amun? Shall we pool our resources to set your boat sailing once more?"

Eyes wide with surprise, Amun bowed to Morris. "Again, sir, you honor me. Let's work together, yes."

Rolling her eyes, Marceline said, "Again, Morris, you frustrate me. Show me how I can help."

Less than an hour passed before the group rode out aboard the sand boat. It hissed and clanked. Its treads crunched rock and grit. Its ceramic skids whispered over the dusty ground. Amun drove, while Morris watched the pressure gauges and dials indicating engine integrity, satisfied with the hasty repair work he and Amun had executed. Marceline reclined, trying to look indifferent while failing to fully suppress a smile revealing that she enjoyed the ride. A ready threat to enemies, the Protectors clung to the sides of the boat. Soon they passed outside the city limits onto open sand, gliding up and down dunes with remarkable steadiness as the pyramids grew in the distance.

The steam engine's throbbing growl kept them from chatting, but Morris found himself speechless anyway, absorbed by the magnificence of the ancient structures ahead, unable to switch off his analytic brain, delving of its own accord into how such lasting tombs were built by people with only stone, sticks, ropes, and muscle at their disposal. His own city measured its age in a fraction of how long the pyramids had stood. He wondered what a visitor might find there four thousand years from now.

The engine sputtered and their smooth travel skipped as the sand boat jolted. Morris glanced at the dials and gauges, which registered a brief pressure surge before settling back to normal. Amun waved off any concern, and they continued on their way. Morris studied the dials more closely now, noting how every so often they jumped almost to the red zone then dropped back. Their makeshift fixes would last only so long. They would arrive in time to meet Lateef, but they might not return to Giza without walking part of the way.

As the sand boat descended a high dune, Morris forgot all about engines and machinery.

Amun steered the sand boat east toward the Great Sphinx and the Pyramid of Khufu. Remnants of the white limestone exterior looked like bleached bones in the sun. A sensation of awe welled up inside Morris. For a moment, he felt like an explorer sailing down a mythical river into the ancient past. Then Marceline took his hand in hers and kissed him on the cheek, and Morris squeezed her fingers in his.

They passed the Sphinx then turned onto a trail along a cemetery toward a row of mastabas, long, flat-roofed stone tombs that resembled benches for giants. They stood arrayed near the base of Khufu's pyramid. The sun, now low in the sky, created an awkward grid of light and shadow, dominated by the sharp silhouette of the pyramid. The sand boat drove toward the funerary temple between the pyramid and the cemetery, halting beside several small pyramids on the cemetery perimeter. Amun flipped switches and pulled levers. The engine gave out a massive dragon's hiss and ejected a long mane of steam as it vented excess pressure then fell into a steady boil on standby for a fast exit. The three Protectors leapt to the sand.

"This place," Morris said. "I have no words."

"Even growing up here, learning their history all my life, hearing people speak of them as commonplace things, I felt what you feel now the first time I saw the pyramids," Amun said. "They are a rare, tangible link to the people we were near the dawn of modern history."

"They are, indeed, magnifique," Marceline said.

Amun gestured toward the nearest of the small pyramids. "Lateef awaits us in the shadow of the pyramid of Queen Meritetis."

Led by one Protector, followed by the other two, they ambled over stone and sand. The sun dipped low, leading toward twilight. Morris noted the relative absence of anyone else among the ancient landmarks. A few visitors wandered on the far side of Khufu's pyramid, and in the distance to the west stood a tent camp, probably home to archeologists and historians. They came around the front of Queen Meritetis's pyramid, and in its shadow stood a man verging on old age, garbed in a light flowing gallibaya and white turban. His long gray beard fluttered in the breeze.

"Lateef, it is good to see you, old friend," Amun said. He introduced Morris and Marceline, whom Lateef greeted with a respectful bow.

"Let us step inside the first chamber of the tomb, away from prying eyes." Lateef cast a warning eye at the Protectors. "What I have to say is only for the four of us."

The trio agreed and shuffled after Lateef through a short, narrow corridor into the gloomy tomb. A torch burning in a sconce cast uneven light on faded hieroglyphics painted on the walls. Outside, the Protectors guarded the entrance. Morris touched the stone. The figures appeared to move in the flickering torchlight, to look back at him with dark, exaggerated eyes, ghosts from the past noting his intrusion on their resting place.

"I am heartened by your arrival," Lateef said. His hoarse voice echoed like falling sand in the confines of the chamber. "There are many in my country who feel you don't belong here, Mr. Garvey, and many who believe your presence is providential to their wish to send a message to the world."

Morris turned away from the hieroglyphics. "What message?"

"That Egypt does not need foreigners to modernize it," said Lateef.

"Nonsense," Marceline said. "Morris is here merely to consult and share his expertise. We are to return home within a few weeks. We are friendly visitors, no more."

"The ancient ways remain strong, albeit hidden," said Lateef. "Ancient memories of foreign invaders who trampled upon the old ways linger vividly among those like the Cult of Bast. Mr. Garvey's home city bears the name of one of our greatest conquerors, an affront to us all, a return of the first man to conquer the world. But as a pantheon ruled ancient Egypt, so today they rule those who still worship in secret. You have encountered two of these cults today. There are others, followers of Isis and Osiris, of Ra, of Sobek and Sekhmet, of

Horus, Thoth, and Hathor, all vying for the Egypt's soul as it travels into the future. Some, Madame Marie and Mr. Garvey, believe sacrificing you to their deity will capture your power for their vision."

"The Cult of Bast?" Morris said.

"Bast is an ambitious and hungry goddess who wishes one day to feast on the world," said Lateef. "Of course, there are others with simpler desires. Some seek only to demonstrate their strength by sowing chaos and disorder among all the others, especially our present rulers who worship modern gods. Such a stain on those fools would it be for two such famous and highly regarded people to vanish or die while visiting under their hospitality. What shame it will bring them when your bodies are found hacked to pieces at the base of Khufu's pyramid, your flesh ripped by the claws of Set's beast."

Lateef reached into his clothing and produced a weapon that extended steel claws of vaguely canine shape over his fingers.

"Allez! I told you so, Morris. Amun Zaki has led us from one terrible death to another," Marceline said.

"No, it's not true!" Amun said. "Lateef, what is this madness? I've known you since I was a boy and never once did you utter the name of Set. You said you wished to help me, help all of Egypt."

"My master doesn't care if he hears his name spoken by lips as lowly as mine. And I am helping, Amun, helping clear the way for you to rise to prominence, for Egypt to bring back the old ways and the old gods."

In the torchlight, Lateef's eyes flickered like the eyes painted on the ancient walls, another specter of a long-ago world whose beauty and power persisted now only in decaying remnants. Morris saw madness in the man's gaze, a lust for lost things he could never reconcile. For a moment, Morris pitied him, but then he acted, lunging, grabbing Lateef's wrist above the steel claws with his right hand as he thrust his left elbow into the man's face, cracking his nose. Lateef crumpled. Morris snatched the claws from his grip as he fell.

"Lateef, did you think you could murder us all by yourself?" Amun said.

Wiping blood from his swelling nose, Lateef smiled then burst out in hacking laughter, his frail body shuddering. "Oh, no, no, Amun, not by myself, no, of course not."

With the swiftness of smoke, four men entered the chamber from a low passageway. Each wielded a khopesh. Morris observed the now familiar maddened lust in their eyes. Pushing Marceline ahead of him, he raced out of the tomb entrance into the fresh-fallen twilight.

"Run!" he cried.

Amun followed. The three burst onto the sand with Set's four assassins at their heels. They didn't go far. Four more men armed with khopeshes greeted them. No sign of the Protectors of the Way remained.

"We're trapped," Marceline said.

"And abandoned by our guardians," said Morris.

"My friends, I am sorry," Amun said. "I've led you, as Madame Marie feared, from the frying pan into the fire. I never meant for this."

"Oh, shut up, you naïve, head-in-the-clouds traitor," Marceline said. "I will believe you only when I see your body in pieces beside mine."

Lateef emerged from the tomb. The eight assassins circled Morris, Marceline, and Amun, and ushered them back the way they had come. The sun had fully set. Beginning its journey across the sky, the arc of the moon gleamed from behind the tip of Khufu's pyramid. The sand boat shimmered in nascent lunar glow. Brass and steel gleamed like ice. Steam wisps swirled in faerie dances. Morris gauged how fast he could get the vehicle moving if he broke away from their captors but saw no scenario for success. It would take too long for sufficient pressure to build.

For the second time that day, a falcon's cry disrupted his captivity. Two others sounded in reply.

"The Protectors didn't forsake us," Amun said. "They only waited because they are more powerful at night, Khonshu's domain."

Lateef sneered. "Three Protectors of the Way against eight of Set's faithful? Their dismembered bodies shall join yours at the foot of Khufu's monument."

The assassins tightened their circle. Six faced outward for the expected attack. Lateef and two others turned inward to watch their prisoners. The moon cleared the pyramid's peak and splashed its light all around them, nearly as bright as day in its fullness. With a flurry of falcon calls, the Protectors attacked. A riot of motion exploded, crook and flail against khopesh, men whirling in a dance of death that filled the air with the noise of violence. One of the Protectors charged into the circle, his strength unmatched by any single opponent. He approached Morris, and said, "Seek Khonshu's light!" before a blade found his back. The circle broke then. In a moment of chaos, Morris found himself pressed against the sand boat.

A bright flash caught his eye. Moonlight reflected off the glass covers of the boat's dials like a spotlight. *Khonshu's light.* The needles bobbed, bobbed, bobbed, then flicker-surged toward the red zone before dropping back to place. Morris reached in, flipped two levers, adjusted the controls, then kicked at part of the engine beneath the sand boat's body closing the steam channels he'd reengineered to the front mechanisms.

Lateef seized Morris and shoved his steel claws against his neck. "Come. Your Protectors are gone, and we must kill you now."

Morris glanced around at the awful evidence of Lateef's words. The Protectors lay dead in the sand, their silver-white clothes stained with blood turned black by moonlight, their limbs hacked from their torsos in honor of Set who had dismembered his brother Osiris. Only three assassins remained, proof that night gave strength to Khonshu's worshippers, though not enough.

Lateef led them to the pyramid. The three surviving assassins took up a position, one by each of their captors. The sand boat gurgled and rumbled. Amun cast Morris a confused look.

"What's that noise?" Lateef turned to face the boat. "That damn machine. We'll leave it here in pieces with you. You can reassemble it for your trip through the Duat."

The assassins raised their khopeshes. The sand boat hummed, blurped, and jolted.

"Marcy, Amun, I suggest we all kneel and turn our backs," Morris said.

"Non, Morris, if I am to die, I will face my killer," Marceline said.

"It's my hope that none of us will die," said Morris. "Kneel, turn, do your best to tuck yourself behind one of these stones." The sand boat boiler chugged. The vehicle shook and vibrated. "Now, do it, now!"

Morris dropped to his knees, spun around, and pushed himself into a cranny between two stone blocks fallen from loose from pyramid's base. He saw Amun and Marceline follow suit and hoped they found equally good cover. The sand boat boiler, its primary stream channel jammed, its integrity weakened by Morris's and Amun's makeshift repairs, groaned—then burst from a pressure overload. The ground shook. The report thundered among the ancient burial ruins. Brass and steel fragments showered the air, deadly rain that elicited cries of anguish from Set's assassins. Only Lateef stayed silent. Not until the resounding explosion faded and shrapnel stopped falling, did

Morris lift up his head to see why. Lateef, decapitated by a sliver of metal, had had no chance to scream.

The mangled remains of the sand boat occupied a steam-clouded crater. Morris helped Marceline to her feet. Amun joined them. Together the three observed the carnage. Amun bent and picked up an intact lever from the sand boat and showed it to Morris with an expression of loss on his face.

"My apologies, Amun," Morris said he stared at the brass part, "If this is what happens when I meddle in Egyptian affairs, however, perhaps it will be proof enough for Mayor Eskander that Egypt's future is best left in Egyptian hands."

Justice Runs Like Clockwork

Christine Norris

"Where you goin'! Ya can't go out dressed like that, the Wardrobe Mistress will have yer hide! Priscilla!"

Priscilla ignored Ann's warning as she ran out the stage door, her hat askew and her coat flapping behind her. Once she reached the sidewalk, she pulled her coat around her to hide her ridiculous outfit.

But there was no help for it, she was running late.

She paused for just a moment to consult the small, gold timepiece pinned to her coat. It was nearly midnight but that meant little in the Quarter. While the Butcher's Market, including Priscilla's favorite beignet stand, was shuttered and dark, the theaters had just closed, and the taverns were still open. If anyone worried about the battle raging downriver at Forts St. Philip and Jackson, it wasn't evident by the mood of the city. Music and lights spilled onto the street at intervals. Plenty of folks walked the sidewalks. Languages blended together here—English, Spanish, French, Creole, German, Irish, all overlaid by African dialects too numerous to count, spoken by the free Africans that remained in the city.

Just another night in New Orleans.

Priscilla pulled her coat around her, though the night was almost too warm for it. The outfit was designed to attract attention, but attention wasn't what she needed right now. The red corset was laced tightly, while the hem of her striped satin skirt swung dangerously high above her ankles. She had managed to exchange her feathered headdress for a black pork pie hat, and dancing slippers for practical boots, before she bolted out of the stage door.

Priscilla wore a face of friendly openness but was acutely aware of her surroundings. The men that passed her, on their way home or to the next party. A man in a Confederate gray officer's uniform, his hat askew, passed Priscilla on the arm of a paid companion. The woman bobbed her head at Priscilla, and she returned in kind. Just two working, solitary women making their way in the world. The woman brushed by Priscilla, and no one, certainly not the officer, noticed the bit of paper passed from the companion to the chorus girl and slipped into the latter's pocket.

"What do we have here? A little girl out after curfew?"

Priscilla paid no mind to the drunken soldier leaning against the building on the corner. She made to cross the street but was stopped by a hand gripping her wrist.

"Are you lost, sweetheart? Stay and have a drink with me."

Priscilla let out an exasperated sigh. "No, thank you."

The man leaned in, his breath rank on her cheek. "Wasn't a request." The man pulled her toward him, and before he took his next breath, she had driven the palm of her free hand up into his nose. The man pulled back, screaming and holding his damaged and bleeding face. "You bith!" he shouted, his words coming out muddied by the injury. "You'll pay for that."

In a blink, Priscilla had her Aether gun free from her thigh holster and pointed at the man. "We're not going to have a problem, are we?"

The man looked at the weapon, his eyes wide. He backed away and shook his head.

"That's what I thought. Have a pleasant evening."

Priscilla left the man bleeding all over Bourbon Street and walked North on St. Louis. The quiet here dropped over her like a blanket. She started to run, her footfalls echoing off of the stately homes that lined the block. She crossed Basin, feeling an almost palpable sensation as she left the French Quarter. The gates of the St. Louis cemetery loomed above her, the night lit by a nearly full moon.

Priscilla paused and made sure she hadn't been followed before pulling open the gate. It announced her arrival with a groan of metal hinges, and she stepped inside the City of the Dead. Tombs of various size and ornateness lined both sides of the path. Mist lay low across the ground, making the place live up to its reputation of nightly ghostly activities.

Priscilla's heart leapt and she suppressed a shiver — nothing here could harm her, but this place always had a heavy air that left her feeling uneasy.

Down one row and up another, a left turn and a right. She had memorized the safe path and knew how to avoid the alarm sensors. Wouldn't do to set one off, not tonight.

She stopped in front of a modest mausoleum in the heart of the cemetery. The name across the top had been engraved into the marble and then purposefully faded so as not to draw any attention to the fact it was less than a year old. Likewise, the stone had been deliberately chipped and rubbed with ash. Priscilla shook back the sleeve of her coat and pulled off her glove. She swung one of the *fleur-de-lis* on the wall of the tomb upward, revealing a set of three numbered dials. She rolled each to the appropriate number and pushed the button beneath them.

Below the fake family name were the names of three invented family members supposedly buried inside. An iris opened in the capital O of Olivia, Dearest Wife and Mother, revealing a smooth bit of thick glass. Priscilla pressed her thumb to the glass. Something *clicked* within, and then the sound of gears and pulleys working. The door swung inward, and a soft glow emanated from within.

"Thank you, Agent Clemens," Priscilla muttered as she pulled on her glove and stepped inside. Beyond it was a tightly wound circular staircase. She stepped on the top stair, and the door pulled itself shut. Gas lamps dotted the wall at regular intervals along the stair, and Priscilla held the polished wooden rail to keep her balance.

Fifteen feet below ground, she entered a stone-lined tunnel that ran both North and South as far as she could see. She pulled her coat tighter to stave off the underground damp and walked North, toward Lake Pontchartrain.

This tunnel extended from the Mississippi to the lake, with the cemetery entrance between. There were other tunnels that connected to it, a system that stretched beneath the city and beyond, including past the fortifications at Chalmette.

The silence of the tunnel was marred by the sound of her boots against the brick floor, and the soft *whirring* of the pumps that kept the tunnel free from the water that constantly tried to pour into the void. The water was then turned to steam which powered the pumps, the lights, and all their necessary equipment. It was a feat of engineering that Priscilla marveled at every time she came down here.

Priscilla slowed her steps, then hopped over a section of brickwork, slightly darker than the rest. To the casual observer, the bricks merely looked damp, but beneath them was a pressure plate that would trigger a stream of lethal gas directly onto the unsuspecting trespasser. There were two more traps on her route, which she skirted easily.

A quarter of a mile from the staircase, Priscilla stopped at a single oak door set in the brick wall. There was no knob, only another smooth oval of thick glass in the center, trimmed with plain brass. Once more, Priscilla pressed her thumb to the plate. With a few *clicks* and *whirrs*, the door swung open.

Headquarters was the size of a ballroom, but with the low ceiling of a cave. A huge oak table sat in the center, with maps spread across almost every available space. Another map was fixed to one wall, with pins stuck into strategic points across the city. Beneath it stretched a long workbench, strewn with tools, instruments, and various odd items. At one end sat a telegraph. The opposite wall was covered with shelves, filled with an assortment of clothing, food, and weapons. Three more people walked about, studying pages of information and searching the shelves.

"It's about time," said a young man who leaned over the table. He did not look at Priscilla.

She glanced at her watch. "What? I'm... two minutes late. I was unavoidably held up. Were you not going to wait for me, Tom?"

Tom tore his gaze from the map and looked Priscilla up and down. "What *are* you wearing?"

Priscilla pulled the pins from her hat and left it on the small table beside the door. "I didn't have time to change after the last performance." She paused, mostly for dramatic effect but also to make sure Tom was paying attention. "Lovell was in the audience tonight."

Her words had the desired effect. Tom straightened and crossed his arms. "Alone?"

Priscilla relished knowing something he didn't. "No. Breckenridge was with him, as well as Mitchell. Along with some lower-ranking officers I didn't recognize."

Tom nodded. "Interesting. Taking in a show, while their Navy fights to hold the river? Overconfidence has always been one of Lovell's more charming character flaws. That group sounds like a real brain trust, especially since Lovell and Mitchell can't stand each other. Wonder what they talked about over dinner?"

Priscilla smiled. "Lovell complained about the lack of ships defending the port. He's still angry that most of the gunships are upriver. Both of them agreed that Whittle is sitting on his hands regarding the *Louisiana* and the rest of the promised Ironclads."

Tom smiled. "However did you get that information?"

Priscilla shrugged and feigned innocence. "Suffice it to say, the waiters at Lovell's club are not all loyal to the Confederate cause."

"I hope you compensated him for his service?"

Priscilla grinned. "You'll never know."

Tom rubbed his hands together in glee. "Excellent work. Anything else to report?"

Priscilla pulled the bit of paper the companion had handed her on Bourbon Street. "Sarah sent this." She handed it to Tom.

"Fantastic. Looks like almost everything is in place." He folded the paper, then held it over the lamp beside him. The paper caught fire, and he dropped it to the ground where it burned to ash. Tom stomped it out then looked at the door. "Where is Jack? He was supposed to be here by now."

"I have no idea," Priscilla replied. "Perhaps he's gotten held up at the waterfront? Or, heaven help us, he's been caught." She didn't want to say that out loud, but it was a possibility for any of them.

"Fortunately for you all, none of the above." The door opened and in stepped a tall, muscular, African man. He shook hands with Tom as he removed his bowler hat. "Everything is ready. However, I was followed tonight, which is the reason for my tardiness."

Tom scowled. "Who? And, of course, you lost them, or you wouldn't be here."

Jack nodded. "Some idiot private who spotted me near the docks decided to harass me. He just adored my gorgeous complexion. Got it in his head I needed to be sent to a cotton field somewhere. Followed me through the Quarter. Tried to lose him, but in the end..." he shrugged. "He won't be a problem."

Priscilla shuddered, for more than one reason. There was a distasteful element to spy craft that couldn't be avoided. This was indeed enemy territory, especially for men and women like Jack.

Jack joined Tom at the table. "Everything in place, then?"

"As long as you did your job, yes." Tom waved everyone over to the table. He pointed to a spot on the map, just downriver. "Farragut has been slinging mortars at Fort St. Philip and Fort Jackson for days, with little success. Captain Labrador is helping with that as we speak." Tom ran his finger along the map, tracing the route of the Mississippi. "Once Farragut gets past, it should be smooth sailing up here to the city. We need to be ready."

Priscilla only knew about her part of the plan, nothing else. She had been told it was for security. No one knew everything except Tom. That way if anyone was captured, they couldn't give too much away.

Jack nodded. "Once the fleet gets here, there will be panic, for certain. If Lovell commands the evacuation of the city, that will only add to it."

"Confusion, in this case, would be a huge help. But I aim to be finished by the time he gets here." Tom straightened and wiped his palms on his pants, then consulted his wristwatch. "Time to go." The three other spies, whose names Priscilla never knew, gathered up their things and disappeared out the door.

Tom moved to the workbench. "You might want to change." His suggestion was tossed over his shoulder at Priscilla.

Priscilla put on a look of mock offense, her hand to her bosom. "What, you don't think this ensemble is inconspicuous enough? Alright, fine." She flounced off to the shelves, where she selected a rough woven shirt, a boy's vest and jacket, and a cap. Taking a moment to switch her timepiece from her own coat to the jacket, she pinned it to the inside so it wouldn't be noticed.

With new clothing acquired, she slipped behind a screen that had been set in the corner to change. The soft fabric and lack of boning in everything allowed her to breathe and move freely. *Men have it so much better. I'd like to see any of them work while wearing a corset and skirt.* Her costume she folded neatly and put aside. She would return it as soon as she was able, and make some excuse about taking it home to remove a stain, or some such.

Using a small mirror on the wall, she tucked her hair beneath the cap. Finally, she secured her weapons—the Aether gun, plus the two knives she always kept on her person—then joined Jack and Tom at the table.

Tom looked up at her approach. "Much better. Just needs a few accessories." He walked to the shelves and took down a pair of goggles, a few spherical objects, a small handheld device, and a leather satchel.

He handed everything to Priscilla, the goggles last. "Don't put these on until you're outside, remember."

"I remember, thanks." Priscilla put the device in her vest pocket and the spheres in the satchel, then she draped the long strap over her shoulder and set the goggles on her head. "Where's the Disruptor? I'm going to need it."

Tom turned back to the workbench and grabbed something that looked like a screwdriver with buttons, to anyone who didn't know better. He handed it to Priscilla, who slipped it into the satchel. "Jack, do you have everything you need?"

Jack took another Disruptor from the workbench and slipped it into his jacket pocket. "All set."

"Hopefully we'll hear something from—" Tom was interrupted by a rapid series of clicks from the telegraph behind him. He ran to the machine. Beside it was a stack of paper and a pencil, and Tom grabbed the top sheet. Licking the end of the pencil, he listened closely for a moment, then began scribbling on the paper. Once the clicking stopped, he put his finger on the knob and tapped out a reply. When he finished, he lifted the paper and turned to his two compatriots.

"It's from the captain. Farragut is in place. He's just waiting on our signal." Tom crumpled the paper and held it over the flame of the lamp beside him.

"You two get going. Things are going to move fast from here on in. Remember your training and keep to your timetable."

Priscilla and Jack nodded.

"And good luck."

Priscilla's last image of Tom before she shut the door was him hunched over the telegraph, tapping out another message.

Priscilla pressed the button that opened the door to the tunnel. The gears and pulleys echoed around the small landing, making her reflexively cringe and suck in a breath. The door slid back into the wall, taking with it the bookshelf on the other side that disguised the entrance. A dark open space greeted her. She pulled the googles over her eyes and pressed a button on the side. In a moment, a modest sitting room of a house in the Quarter came into view. The room also served as a beauty parlor, and when the need arose, a séance room. Priscilla stepped away from the wall and the bookcase slid silently back into place.

She slipped through the room easily, ignoring the pots of unusual spices and oddly labeled jars. She crept past the front room and its full altar, covered with colored candles and charms for luck, money, and love. Marie, the woman who lived here and a so-called "Voodoo Queen" was an ally, despite putting on all appearances of being a good Catholic and loyal to the Confederacy. Meanwhile, she funneled information to Priscilla, and was one of many who assisted in hiding and sending slaves to freedom.

Priscilla shut the front door behind her and started on her way. The night-seeing goggles made it easy for her to stick to the shadows as she walked back through the Quarter. The parties had ended, finally, and the streets were empty save for the stray cats of New Orleans. She crossed the streets listening to their nightly opera.

Ahead of her, the St. Louis Hotel stood tall and majestic, the lavish architecture a monument to New Orleans' love of decadence. It took up an entire block. A glass dome rose in the center, though it was too dark to see it. A shiver crawled up Priscilla's spine. When she had first come to New Orleans, just four years ago, she had walked inside the St. Louis, looking for work. The day had burned itself into her memory. She had followed the crowd, all seemingly excited for something. They had gathered under the dome, pressing in around the edges of the circular room, clearly anticipating whatever would happen in the center, where several wooden stages had been placed. Once the "event" had started, an auction, to be precise, Priscilla's stomach churned, and she was barely able to contain her scream of horror as she raced from the building. Since then, she had discovered how many other places in the city held similar events, almost daily. That's when she knew she would fight until her last breath to end such abhorrent practices.

And tonight her… *their* efforts would come to conclusion.

She pushed her goggles back, tucked herself in a doorway across from the colonnaded entrance and checked her watch by the light of the streetlamps. *Any second now.*

Off in the distance, she heard a low-pitched *whoomph*. If it had been day and the streets full of people, the sound might have been missed altogether. But the sound of a sonic torpedo from Captain Labrador's submarine was unmistakable.

The device Tom had given her vibrated in her vest pocket. She pulled out the tiny machine Tom liked to call the Mini Telegraph. It operated in a similar way, except that instead of taps, this gave little vibrations, which translated to Morse code. It was wireless, another of the ingenious inventions the Resistance's engineers had developed. She held it in her palm and felt the message.

Chain has been breached. Proceed.

When it had repeated twice, she nodded and slipped it into her pocket.

Captain Labrador had succeeded in taking down the chain the Confederates had strung across the river. The last obstacle between the Union Navy and New Orleans had been circumvented. Priscilla pulled the Disruptor from her pouch and made a last check of the street. She turned the end of the device, and it hummed in her hand.

Five... four... three... two...

The streetlights blinked out, dropping the street into darkness. *Right on time.* Priscilla pulled her goggles back over her eyes and the world came into sharp focus. Leaning out from her hiding spot, she scanned the area. Darkness shrouded the entire Quarter. She stepped into the middle of the street, aimed the Disruptor at the hotel's front door, and held her breath as she pressed the button.

The Disruptor let out a high-pitched squeal, its invisible waves finding and detonating the devices that Jack had placed inside earlier today. The building muffled the boom, not nearly as satisfying as she had hoped. Jack's bombs had been meant to only damage the rotunda, leaving minimal damage to the rest of the structure. The slave auction was demolished.

Priscilla didn't stop to admire her work. There was more to do before the night was over. She ran to the end of the block, the hotel's second-floor balcony shielding her from view of anyone who had heard the blast and might come to investigate. More explosions in the distance made her pause to listen for just a moment. Every slave auction in the city was being blasted to Kingdom Come. With a grin, she turned the corner and scurried along the side of the hotel. Halfway down was an alley that ran behind the hotel, holding the St. Louis' carriage houses and stables. Priscilla raced down it until she found the entry she wanted. She turned the dial on the Disruptor to a new setting, pushed the button, and the padlock fell to the ground.

When she pulled the doors open, the scent of unwashed humans nearly overwhelmed her. As she scanned the pens inside, her nausea increased. Every pen was filled, with ten or more slaves stuffed inside. Men, women, children.

"Hello? Um, I've come to get you out of here."

No one moved. Priscilla realized that she could see them, but they couldn't see her. They stood to the back of the pens, huddled together, some shaking in fear.

She made her voice as gentle as possible. "I know this must be terrifying, but we have to get out of here before someone comes to see what's going on. I promise I'm here to help you."

Again, no one moved, as the whimpers of children floated in the dark.

"Most of them don't understand you. And we can't see you."

The voice came from the back of the barn, a deeper, male-sounding voice. "They don't speak English."

Priscilla followed the sound. The speaker pushed his way to the front of the pen. He was tall, well-muscled, and looked healthy. His eyes moved back and forth, searching for her face in the dark.

Priscilla gave a useless nod. "Unfortunately, I don't speak anything else. My French is atrocious at best, and I couldn't begin to know any of their native dialects." She grabbed a lantern from the wall and lit it. "Your English is very good." She didn't hear any kind of accent, and wondered where the man was from, but now wasn't the time to ask.

The man ignored her comment. He glanced at his fellow captives. "You're really here to help?"

"Absolutely, but we have to be fast or else this will get... messy." Priscilla aimed the Disruptor at the pen's lock. "Back away from the door."

The man murmured to the people in the pen as he shuffled them back. She used the Disruptor once again. There was a high-pitched sound, and the lock popped open. Priscilla pulled it off and opened the gate.

"Get them to the street, I'll get the rest." She handed the lantern to the man who had spoken. "Do not light any more lanterns, darkness is our ally right now."

"Who are you?" the man asked.

"It's better that you don't know," Priscilla answered. "Just know that I'm a friend."

The man took the lantern and nodded. "Gabriel."

Gabriel turned to the people and gestured for them to follow. In less than a minute, Priscilla had all the pens open. People spilled into the barn and through the open front door. When they were clear, she reached into her satchel and took a few of the spheres Tom had given her. She tossed one into the straw of each pen at the back of the barn. Then she pulled out her Aether gun and fired once at each sphere. As the devices exploded, the straw caught fire. Smoke began to fill the barn.

"That will keep them busy."

Priscilla turned to make her exit, then stopped. Above the sound of the flames was another, small sound. She looked around, her goggles becoming less useful as the fire brightened the room.

"Hello? Anyone there?"

She swept the pens, searching. It was soft but sounded like weeping. Smoke filled the barn, making Priscilla cough and her eyes water. She was almost out of time, but something told her she needed to keep looking.

In the corner of one pen, a child lay curled in a ball, shivering in terror. Priscilla raced into the pen and scooped her up. The child clutched something to her body — a small orange kitten.

In the time it had taken Priscilla to find the child, the fire had grown rapidly. It raced up one of the barn's support beams and across the roof. Pieces of wood fell to earth, barely missing them. She lost her bearings, her eyes watering and her lungs filling with smoke. The child coughed in her arms, and Priscilla's heart pounded. *Where is the damn door?*

A shape appeared ahead of her, and then Gabriel was there. He grasped her by the elbow and pulled her through the smoke. After a dozen steps the air began to clear a bit, seeming lighter and slightly cleaner.

They were just feet from freedom when Priscilla heard the loud groaning above her. Gabriel shoved her and the child forward, and she stumbled into the alley. Someone, she couldn't see who, took the girl and her kitten, and Priscilla turned around just in time to see the roof collapse.

Crashing down on Gabriel. Flames engulfed the inside of the barn.

Time stood still, and the world came into sharp focus. Behind Priscilla rose gasps and cries of shock. In front of her, heat and flame erased the man that had saved her life. Her heart leapt into her throat. She wanted to race into the barn, but knew it meant her own life, and there were people counting on her.

"He gave his life to save yours, don't waste his sacrifice!" Whether they understood or not, she didn't have time to find out. Bells clanged in the distance, fire engines likely coming to see about the smoke. Those companies would be busy tonight.

Priscilla waved her hands, indicating they should follow and be quick and quiet. A few of the men spoke quietly to those around them, and the message spread rapidly. She felt the mood shift as they all looked at her expectantly.

"All right, then. This way."

She led the group of men, women, and children to the end of the alley. She stopped at the corner to listen. More bells, and the sound of men shouting.

"Quiet and quick as you can. Stay together."

The message was relayed as they stepped onto the street. Priscilla shuttled them up one street and down another. Twice she had to change course to avoid the fire brigade, and once for a group of soldiers.

They came to the edge of the Quarter and crossed into Treme. Priscilla allowed herself to feel a bit of relief. Treme was a neighborhood made of mostly free African folk. The houses were less grand and closer together, but it was by far safer than the Quarter. The night remained quiet and dark, and anyone peeking through their curtains wouldn't tell what they saw. Priscilla used her goggles to scan the area as they made their way past sleeping houses toward freedom.

Shouts and the baying of dogs sounded behind them, closer than expected. Someone had discovered the missing slaves. Priscilla dodged down an alley, thirty people behind her, and motioned for quiet. Her charges didn't need to be told twice. They huddled together while Priscilla scoped out the other end of the alley and the street beyond. It was clear, but the shouts and dogs were even closer. There, at the end of the next block — a regiment of soldiers, their gray uniforms blending in with the dark, the lights of their lanterns like phantoms bobbing as they walked.

Priscilla slipped a hand into her satchel and pulled out the last of the explosive spheres and a pair of small, mechanical wings. Her hands were steady as she attached the wings to the grenade and wound the wings' mechanism. She released it, and the grenade silently lifted into the air. With a gentle push from Priscilla, it flew down the street. She tracked its path in the dark, and when it was two blocks in the opposite direction she needed to go, she took careful aim with the Aether gun and fired.

The grenade's blast did minimal damage, but it was enough to distract their pursuers. The shouts turned away, growing distant.

Priscilla shepherded her charges out of the alley, and they silently slipped away.

Five more blocks of tense sneaking, and Priscilla brought the group to a halt. The house looked like every other house on the street—an unassuming but well-kept clapboard cottage with a small porch and dormer windows on the upper half-story.

The only difference between it and its sisters was the single lantern burning in the front window.

Priscilla led them around the back. A Haitian woman, her hair wrapped in a colorful scarf, waited for them.

"Praise be!" the woman whispered. "When I heard the dogs, I was so afraid!"

"So was I," Priscilla whispered back. She took the woman's hand in hers. "Cécile, we can't thank you enough."

"It is so little, compared to what is at stake." Cécile waved away the thanks and shooed them toward the backyard.

The tidy yard was barely more than a patch of dirt. At the far end stood a small shed with what looked to be a plain wooden door. Priscilla once again used her thumbprint to unlock it and open the door, which was revealed to be three-inch-thick metal. Beyond it, a shaft dropped straight down into the dark, navigated by a ladder bolted to the far wall. She found one of the men who understood English and asked him to lead everyone down the shaft and wait for her there.

The group murmured among themselves, and some sounded frightened. Priscilla understood. They had followed her up until this point, but now she was asking them to go somewhere they couldn't see, into a small, cramped space. It must bring up bad memories for many.

Cécile moved among them, speaking her own Creole language in low tones, then repeating her words in other languages Priscilla didn't comprehend. Heads began to bob, and then they descended, single-file.

Priscilla didn't remember to breathe until the last child and her kitten had descended, then she exhaled in a rush and started toward the ladder. The Union Navy was on its way, and the city may very well soon descend into chaos, but she had completed this part of her mission.

Someone put a hand on her shoulder.

Priscilla spun, her Aether gun taking aim, her finger on the trigger.

Gabriel jumped back and held up his hands in a gesture of surrender. Priscilla lowered her weapon.

"What? How? I saw you get crushed by a roof. That was on fire."

Gabriel shook his head. "It doesn't matter." There was something behind his eyes, a secret, perhaps. Definitely more to the story than he was willing to share even if there were time.

She ushered Gabriel into the shed and descended the ladder. At the bottom, her boots landed on the solid floor of one of the spy network's tunnels. It was wider than the others, lanterns casting spots of light that led farther than she could see. In the center of the tunnel lay a train track.

Priscilla snaked her way through the milling crowd and came out by the track's terminus. Sitting there, waiting for them like a sleeping beast, sat a small steam engine. Three open cars were hooked to the rear, with cushioned benches on either side. Steam billowed from beneath the engine, and smoke from the stack, which was pulled out of the tunnel by an air shaft overhead.

Jack leaned against the engine, his crooked smile growing wide as Priscilla approached. "Excellent work."

Priscilla accepted the praise with a nod of her head. "We're not done yet." She turned toward her charges, who once again looked terrified. She looked around for Gabriel and found him right behind her.

"Help me get them loaded?"

"Where are we going?" Gabriel's tone held no suspicion.

"To freedom," Jack replied. "Out of the city, where the next leg of the journey awaits." He tilted his head and looked at Gabriel. "Where are you from, anyway?"

Gabriel hesitated, then shrugged. "Philadelphia. There are a few of us here, free men kidnapped in the North and dragged here like animals. I was jumped in an alley, the next thing I knew I was on a boat headed here."

Jack nodded. "Not an uncommon story, my friend. But one that is about to take a turn for the better." He and Gabriel shook hands, then together they spoke to the group. The gathered former slaves climbed aboard the rail cars, settling on the comfortable seats. For many, their postures relaxed for the first time since their escape. A few even managed to smile.

"This is where we say goodbye," Priscilla said to Gabriel. She held out her hand. "Moses will meet you at the next stop. Keep their spirits up, it isn't an easy journey."

Gabriel took it and shook it firmly. "I thank you. And these people thank you."

Priscilla's heart swelled. "Doing my job. You know, you seem pretty resourceful. You'd make a good agent."

Gabriel laughed. "Not on your life." He walked backward, toward the last car. With a small salute, he pulled himself up and into a seat.

Jack jumped in the engine and released the brakes. As the train slowly pulled away, everyone waved to Priscilla as they passed, gifting her with grateful and happy smiles. She stood in the tunnel and watched until she could no longer hear the train.

"Good luck and good life." She spun on her heel and climbed up the ladder.

This night was not over for her. Back to work.

Author's note: *New Orleans was one of the largest slave trade cities of the Confederacy, and the St. Louis Hotel and Exchange was one of the busiest slave markets in the city, though the auction usually occurred in the lobby, not the rotunda. This came to an end (mostly) when the Union Navy and Admiral David Farragut landed in the city during the Battle of New Orleans, April 25-May 1, 1862.*

Mark Twain (aka: Samuel Clemens) was one of the first people to understand that fingerprints were unique to individual people, as seen in his memoir, "Life on the Mississippi."

The "reverse Underground Railroad" was real; Africans in the North were often kidnapped and sent to New Orleans to be sold at the slave market.

Moses was the code name for Harriet Tubman.

ON THE WINGS OF AN ANGEL

DANIELLE ACKLEY-McPHAIL

CAN'T SAY AS I DIDN'T RECKON I WAS GOING MAD. IT WOULDN'T HAVE surprised me if'n it were so. I already reckoned I was in hell, that's enough to turn anyone's mind…

But first, I call myself Miss Sadie Angelina Carlisle, though I don't bother much with any name but the middle one anymore. Not since takin' up residence at the Lucky Strike Saloon in Dead Dog, Montana, anyway. See, the proprietor, Mr. Clayton, he says men are happier pretendin' they're keepin' company with an angel, rather than a common whore. I do as I'm told, else Mr. Clayton might forget he likes havin' an angel below stairs temptin' and teasin' the custom, rather than just another girl entertainin' above stairs. Men don't pay near so much for common. They have to save up for an angel, even a fallen one; unless they hit a strike. That ain't happened yet. Till then, I sing.

"Sadie! Sun's settin', quit wool-gatherin' and get yourself into your rig afore I find someone else as fits it!"

Lordie, but that black-hearted Clayton can bellow. I can't help but shudder at his bald-faced threat though. That happen, and I might as well drop the name Angel too. Ain't none of us outta reach of his temper. I'd do to remember that. And I reckon he's been givin' me looks makin' me wonder will I be below stairs much longer anyhow. Looks that make me think he's tired of waitin' for a prospector with that big strike to come along. I've no doubt I've only been spared entertainin' the custom 'cause there ain't anyone come in able to pay the price Mr. Clayton has set on my innocence.

I flinch at the thought and rush to do as I'm bid, my mind near jibberin' half-formed pleas for deliverance, but not hardly expectin' it will ever come. I'm already wearin' my white satin gown and matchin' slippers with the thick leather soles; now for the rest. Quick-like I beckon over Shelby, one of the above stairs ladies, for some help 'cause I plum can't suit up all myself.

See, our Mr. Clayton, he's into mods and mechanicals. Show him somethin' with gears and I reckon he starts breathin' like he's been with a five-dollar whore. There are bits of invention all over the saloon I can scarce make sense of. They're most nothin' much but tinker's toys like the little metal birds what can't fly, but sing pertier than me… if'n only ever just one song, and miniature carriages made for Cook's son movin' by themselves on tiny puffs of steam... The bartender is flesh enough, but there ain't a bottle of liquor to be seen—nor broke, if'n the custom gets rowdy. Drinks is portioned out by a clockwork contraption of gears and pipes that can take a dent and keep on pourin' the next drink in just as precise a measure as the last. Then there's the player piano what plays itself like any other, but ain't no crank involved, just lotsa steam and valves and whatnot. It's an amazin' thing of copper and brass instead of wood, with gold-plated keys, and not soundin' no more tinny than any other upright I ever heard.

But all of that ain't nothin' compared to my rig.

I can't help but think about that with longin' and loathin' mixed, rememberin' when and how it came to be. There were a tinker come through town. An odd, dirt-smudged, little man what made me more nervous than an uncooped hen after dark. The first he scurried into the saloon and looked his fill at every one of us, we felt near stripped bare down to our very souls, though there weren't nothin' to it that was lecherous or mean. More like Mr. Edward S. Curtis, what came through with his pho-tography equipment once on his way to visit the Blackfoot injuns; he used to look just so at near everythin', like he was searchin' for the perfect picture it would make.

I swear if I didn't feel the tinker's gaze linger just the same on me, though I can't fathom why. I was a young'n yet at the time, and nothin' special to catch the custom's eye. Like now, I sang for my place, when I weren't cleanin'.

Was the tinker first called me Angel, with a nervous-makin' gleam in his eye—like he saw more to me than I right knew was there—and him not even knowin' my given name. That amused Mr. Clayton so much it stuck.

Then that there tinker set to catch Mr. Clayton's attention with such contraptions as you can't never imagine and I can scarce describe. The things that came out of his sack… my Lord, it was a sight. The two of 'em spent more'n a piece of time with their heads together, hagglin'. Hard to say who hoodwinked who, but both men walked away with a smarmy smile.

The tinker stayed a spell after. He puttered around in the cellar until near all you heard afore hours was bangin' and the hiss of steam, but evenin's he ended up in the saloon pesterin' me. Askin' questions and starin' me up and down mutterin' "not yet" under his breath, like maybe I didn't quite match the picture in his head.

The questions made me more nervous than the mutterin'. They was dangerous questions: *What did I wish for? What would I rather be?* I was too feared then to speak, but my heart… it was cryin' out to be free! There was nothin' I wanted more than deliverance. The tinker just nodded and gave me a wink, like he heard what I ain't said, before disappearin' again back down to the cellar.

I wanted to believe. Darn near convinced myself he could do anythin' — includin' save me — after seein' him tinker with one of the songbirds what always sang particularly sad. I'd felt my forehead for a fever when he closed up its tiny back and brushed a finger over it what set it glitterin' and glowin' like pixie dust. Then… that little bird took wing, flyin' out the window never again to be seen! It trilled a happy song as it escaped.

A *different* song.

That's when I had to wonder was I goin' mad.

And still, I took to hopin' then, though ain't nothin' ever come of it.

Afore he left for good, that little man cornered me in the pantry whiles I was helpin' Cook with supper. He stood there, hunched and taut, again starin' me up and down all familiar-like. "Don't you worry… for now, you're safer here," he'd murmured, his head side-cocked and his eyes narrowed like he was lookin' again for his own perfect picture. "But remember, when that's no longer so… Angels were made to fly."

His words left me ashiver in a way I declare I'd never felt afore or since.

To this day, I can hear him whisperin' that, and would swear on my dead ma's Bible if'n I had it that I sometimes still spy him in the shadows, watchin', eyes narrowed just so, though I know he's gone. Quite mad, true, I but can't help but wishin' that mayhap the tinker were right and I'll have me a chance to fly away.

Anyhow, by the time the tinker finally moved along after considerable time spent in the cellar, the parlor had acquired somethin' wondrous new.

Even now I can't help but hold my breath whiles Shelby unlocks my special cabinet. The thing is tall, clear up to the above stairs ceilin'. The whole front and sides foldin' back with fancy paintin' everywhere on the inside, like you would imagine heaven to be, all but for what Mr. Clayton calls the new-matic tube; a brass pipe runnin' down the center, shiny as the day the tinker set it in place.

My rig just hangs there in the middle of the air like someone forgot to paint in the angel, 'ceptin' for its halo and wings—I ain't ever yet been tall enough for that halo to perch proper atop my head. Each time I see The Angel it dazzles me, so's I always near forget how much I dread to buckle the contraption on.

Ain't got no choice, though. Never did. Mr. Clayton says an Angel's gotta have wings if'n anyone's gonna believe she fell from heaven.

An' mayhap they do, when I'm singin'—if I can be forgiven the smallest bit of pride. Savin' for my voice, there's precious little about me that ain't common, or so my pa use to say. 'Course given this rig here—and the presence of the above stairs ladies—I'd be a mite surprised did the gents notice a thing about myself, no matter that I'm hoverin' in thin air above their heads lookin' near the picture of angelic. (Times like that, I can't help but remember the tinker's words... and that little metal songbird. My heart goes all tight each time I do...)

Oh glory, just to look at it... Wings made of gen-u-ine swan feathers brushed light like with gold. Mr. Clayton's after callin' it *guilt*, then laughin' his fool ass off like'n he said somethin' funny. Which, given the nature of his establishment...

I'm mighty fond of those perty wings. The corset, though... that there's a pure torment to wear. I must stand just so the entire time if'n I'm to have enough air to breathe, let alone sing as I'm expected. I do imagine were not the whole thing latched on to the new-matic tube I *could* plum fly away. I reckon I wish that were so somethin' fierce.

Right now, the only thing protectin' my virtue is my singin', and my not-quite-generous curves. I'm afeared that won't be so for long bein' I've had to dodge more'n a few grabbin' hands of late.

Before Mr. Clayton can bellow once more, I step up onto the platform makin' up the bottom of the cabinet, and though I mostly feel forsaken, I lift up a prayer to the God my ma once swore by. After all, in a manner, she'd been delivered, even if her passin' had left me to bear pa alone, if'n only for a short spell, before he foisted me off on Mr. Clayton.

I step into the frame, careful of the many danglin' straps and buckles, makin' sure my feet set just so on the narrow brass plate they're meant to perch on. I shudder to recall the time they'd slipped from that square. The breath was near squeezed out of me. I've learned to be particular since. My eyes close all on their own and I draw deep and full till my lungs near want to burst as Shelby cages me in that rig of iron ribbin', white leather, and polished brass. Otherwise there ain't no room to breathe once the contraption's buckled tight.

Those lookin' on see nothin' but perty; from the moment I'm buckled in till they free me, I'm nigh in pain, forced to stand straight and still as Sundy service else scald my back on the gleamin' brass pole behind me.

It was a wonder I could ever sing a note, but derned if I don't put the nightingale to shame each and every night when I put on The Angel and dangle there in 'heaven' to give the custom a show, and that ain't no boast.

I hear the clunk of the lever bein' pulled across the room, followed by the hiss of steam warmin' the ledge beneath my feet. There's the *whir* of shiftin' gears as the wings spread, and I feel just a bit giddy as I rise up in the air above the platform. Can't help but wonder maybe this time I won't stop in the middle. Mayhap I'll be crushed against the ceilin' or, mayhap I'll sure enough fly away. There ain't no holdin' back my giggle at that. But then the sound of the hiss changes and my perch slows, then stops.

I feel it then. A shiver down m'spine. Familiar-like, enough that I expect I'd see him… the tinker… if'n my eyes weren't shut. I imagine I hear that little songbird as well, and I let my eyes drift open to see did either of 'em really come back.

But all that's there is the familiar sight of The Angel framed in the mirror behind the bar. Only not quite the same as always…

Just a tiny gasp escapes me and I forget to look for what I expected.

For the first time ever, that there halo's just behind my head and The Angel's starin' back, all brown-gold curls and creamy white skin, with a tiny waist and a bosom to put the above stairs ladies to shame. She's wearin' my face.

But it ain't that what startles me. It were Mr. Clayton holdin' up a walnut-size nugget of gold with a shit-eatin' grin on his face. Standin' next to him was a grubby, overlarge miner smellin' rank even from here.

No longer able to deny my days of bein' safe were done, I recoil, only to have fierce heat sear my back.

I don't smell scorched satin or burnt flesh, as I'd expect. I smell a garden like my ma use to have, and again I hear that tiny metal bird. The burnin's gone afore I even draw breath to cry out and in the mirror I swear that pipin' hot brass ain't at my back no more.

A gasp rises from every throat in the room and if I weren't so scared I'd laugh as their eyes go wide, but I'm afraid to move, afraid to fall. Then somethin' brushes my shoulders, sends them tinglin' like they been long asleep and only just wakin' up. I start to glitter. I shiver again and a flush steals over me. Wisps of steam curl at my feet like soft white clouds, no longer overwarm. Then… quiet by my ear, barely louder'n a breath… I hear the tinker's sigh-like whisper, "Now… be free."

I feel like I imagine that bird did, afraid to believe… afraid not to.

My body shakes at the tinker's words, in eager like tremors from head to toe. Mayhap I imagine it… mayhap I truly am mad… but somethin' sparks off my skin, rises up from my bones and sets me aglow. I remember the songbird as I feel the sudden flex of wings at my back, the bunchin' of muscles I ain't ever used. I open my mouth and out pours a terrible, wonderful, glorious sound.

As The Angel sings, the buckles fall away, and m'iron cage rains to the sawdust-covered floor in pieces as gilded feathers lift me to the sky.

No One Alone

David Lee Summers

Onofre Cisneros tightened a coupling, then stood back and examined his work. Studying the set of plans beside him, he nodded, satisfied the new engine should function as expected. As he filled a cylinder with potassium chlorate, a knock sounded at the door. "Come in," he called as he screwed a cap on the cylinder.

A woman entered Onofre's workshop. Estrella Mondragón had shoulder-length, black hair, dark brown eyes, and curves he longed to know as intimately as he did the engine before him. "Papá wanted to know if you could help him fix the rudder on his boat?"

"I'd be happy to, but..." Onofre wiped his hands on a rag and fought the urge to step closer. "Should you be here alone, without a chaperone?"

She reached into the folds of her voluminous skirt and revealed a six-gun concealed within, then winked as she returned it to its hidden pocket. "I can chaperone myself, thank you very much, Señor Cisneros. My father wouldn't have it any other way."

"Your ability to defend yourself reassures me." He smiled, then indicated the engine. "Before we go, do you want to see what I've been working on?"

She quirked an eyebrow. "Another invention?"

He shrugged. "Not exactly an invention, but I have made improvements." He went to the small engine, a metallic block about three feet on a side with cylindrical tanks attached. Onofre opened three valves. A *whoosh* sounded as chemicals mixed inside. Within a few minutes, a gurgling started. Pistons began to move and a shaft protruding from underneath the block proceeded to spin.

Onofre clenched his fist and grinned. "It works!"

Estrella took a cautious step toward the engine and examined it. "It looks like a steam engine, but I don't see a firebox or smoke."

"You won't." Onofre pointed to three slender cylinders. "A reaction of potassium chlorate, manganese dioxide, and zinc boils the water. A fairly small amount in a controlled release will keep the engine running for hours."

Estrella narrowed her gaze. "Still, there must be an exhaust port." Estrella had been around boats long enough to have a passing familiarity with steam engines.

Onofre smiled at her and pointed to another cylinder. "There is, and the exhaust is captured here." He turned another valve and a vent hissed. He motioned the gas toward his nose. "Ah! Fresh air."

"The engine's exhaust is just air?"

Onofre closed the engine's valves. "Well, oxygen, but that's much better than smoke, especially if you want to use this engine in a special type of boat."

"What type of boat did you have in mind?"

"A submarine boat." Onofre held his hand toward the heating unit. Once satisfied it no longer generated heat, he grabbed a small toolkit, then led Estrella outside. A brilliant blue sky hung overhead and the Pacific Ocean's waters lapped a nearby beach. They lived in Rancho Ensenada de Santos, a small seaside village in México's Baja California province. So peaceful, unlike much of Onofre's life before he moved there.

"A boat? You're a mining engineer." Estrella stepped closer but refrained from actually touching Onofre, which would be improper.

Onofre glanced around at the mountains that ringed the village. "I *was* a mining engineer, until the Americans opened more profitable operations north of the border."

She waved his words aside. "The important part is that you made good money and that's what would keep me from serving you calabazas should you ask my father for my hand in marriage." When a man proposed marriage, a meal would be served. If the woman served the man squash, it meant the offer had been rebuffed.

Onofre rubbed his neck. In truth, he'd spent most of his money on the engine. "You see… the money won't last. I need to find something sustainable." He held his hand out toward the bay. "If I can build the submarine boat and demonstrate its usefulness, maybe I can find an investor and build more."

She batted her eyelashes at him. "It almost sounds like you would enjoy that, perhaps more than coming home to a señora who loves you very much."

He flashed a charming smile and doffed his hat. "Ah, mi corazón, I am no one alone. Your love would complete me."

Her laugh was more than a flirtatious titter but not an outright guffaw. As far as Onofre could tell, his words struck just the right chord with her. They soon reached the shore and Estrella's father, Arturo, and his first mate, Luis Ramirez, waved from the boat.

"What could you use a… submarine boat for?" Estrella returned to the earlier conversation.

"The Americans would use them for warfare." Onofre shuddered. "But such boats could also be used for exploration or underwater maintenance. I have a complete set of plans from a Spanish inventor. He wanted to use the craft for coral diving, but I can adapt his mechanical arms to clean barnacles off hulls and repair damage without having to bring ships into a dry dock."

"Indeed, it sounds like a profitable endeavor. If anyone could build such a craft, it would be you."

Onofre took Estrella's hand and kissed it, grateful for her faith in him. As he looked up, he noticed Luis watching. Estrella squeezed Onofre's hand, took a few steps away, then blew a kiss in the boat's general direction. With a sigh, Onofre turned and stepped up to Estrella's father.

"Don Arturo, please, show me the problem with the rudder."

"So, what were you and my daughter discussing?" Arturo asked as they bent over the boat.

Onofre told Arturo about the engine as he adjusted rudder's cable tension. "A Spanish inventor named Narcís Monturiol tried to sell plans for a submarine boat to the American military ten years ago. One of the American mining engineers here had worked for the War Department at the time and had a copy of the plans. He saw potential, but didn't quite believe a Spaniard could come up with something superior to American or British technology. He sold the plans to me. I thought if I actually built the boat and showed how it worked, someone might invest in it." He tightened a couple of bolts, then had Arturo try the tiller.

Satisfied that the rudder now worked as it should, Arturo paid Onofre enough for a meal, then went home to have lunch with his daughter. Onofre didn't want to eat alone and knew Luis would have the latest news, so he invited the sailor to join him in the shade of a beachside cantina. They ordered agua frescas to drink and fish tacos for lunch.

Luis leaned forward. "Did you hear about José María Villagrana?"

Onofre shook his head. Villagrana was Baja California's sub-prefect. He also owned shares in an overland freight company that shipped goods to the United States through Tijuana.

"José Moreno forced him to resign," Luis continued. "It's said that Moreno would like to turn Rancho Ensenada into a proper sea port. Maybe your submarine boat would come in handy here."

Onofre considered the possibilities. "Even better, maybe I could convince an American investor to help me develop the port. I could use the money."

Luis narrowed his gaze. "I thought you had money."

"I spent much of it on the plans for the submarine. The rest went into parts." Onofre held up a taco. "What I earn doing odd jobs is just enough to feed me and keep a roof over my head."

Luis looked back toward the rolling waves. "If we get more boats and facilities here, maybe I could be more than Arturo's assistant one of these days."

Onofre sipped his agua fresca and eyed Luis. "Would you like to be his son-in-law?"

Luis sputtered as though a secret had been discovered. "No... no. It's just... I'd like my own boat—maybe even a few boats—one day."

Onofre's stomach sank and he thought perhaps he'd revealed too much about his finances to Luis. He'd never considered the first mate competition for Estrella's hand, possibly because Luis and Estrella had known each other so long and a union hadn't happened yet. For that matter, poor as Onofre was, Luis had even less money. Social standing and personal wealth mattered in México, but those lines sometimes blurred in hard times.

The two friends fell into an uncomfortable silence and finished their meals. As Onofre returned to his workshop, his thoughts turned to the conflicts that seemed to swirl all around him. He had survived America's invasion of México for land and France's invasion for profit. He desperately hoped México could find a peaceful, prosperous future.

He'd been born in a town called Mora, in Nuevo México. American forces attacked twice. The first time, the villagers chased them off. The second time, the Americans literally burned the village to the ground. Onofre's family fled to El Paso del Norte. He still remembered the screams of his cousins and his aunt as soldiers gunned them down.

Later, he studied to be an engineer. As he began his career, the French invaded México, ostensibly to collect debts. He went to work for a French mining company near El Paso. When Republican forces under Benito Juárez attacked French holdings, he escaped to the west coast. Again, memories of gunshots and screams echoed through his thoughts.

He closed his eyes. So much fighting. So much violence. He wanted to build a better future for himself and México.

Just north of the border, Phineas Banning had built a sea port for Los Angeles along with a connection to the Southern Pacific Railroad. He wondered if Banning would invest in a Mexican seaport, especially if he could get plans for an innovative submarine boat in the bargain.

The next day, Onofre took a letter addressed to Phineas Banning to the Rancho Ensenada stagecoach office. Even though he wasn't an especially devout Catholic, he said a prayer to ensure the letter would make it safely across the border and into Banning's hand.

To keep himself occupied, Onofre gathered the parts he would need for the submarine. He traversed the mountains surrounding Rancho Ensenada with a burro-drawn wagon. He went from the Real de Castillo and Los Alamosa Mines north of town to the mines of the Santa Clara Valley to the southeast. He gathered abandoned machinery and timbers. From time to time, he would return home to find that someone wanted to hire Onofre, bringing him much-needed income, but also distracting him from his primary task. After a few days, he realized he needed help.

He asked Luis to round up some friends. Several people answered the call. They both admired Onofre's submarine boat and thought it a strange, new idea. Still, like Onofre, they wanted Rancho Ensenada to prosper. Many had come to work in the mines only to find they had closed.

The project soon grew too big for Onofre's workshop and he used his wagon to carry the assembled pieces to Rancho Ensenada's beach. On one such trip, Arturo invited him to the house for dinner. Onofre looked forward to the opportunity to see Estrella.

"Sounds like you're making good progress on your strange boat," Arturo remarked after they finished eating.

"We are. We're ready to begin assembling the pieces," Onofre said.

Estrella folded her arms and frowned. "I, for one, will be glad when you're done with the submarine boat. I think you're more interested in that boat than me."

Onofre snapped his fingers. "You should come and help us out. We could use more hands and this craft is our future."

She couldn't hide a faint grin. "I'd be delighted." Then she folded her arms. "Are you sure you trust a woman to help?"

Onofre held out his hands. "Mi corazón, I am no one alone. I need all the assistance I can get and it would let us spend more time together—" he glanced at Arturo "—with many eyes to make sure we remain well behaved, of course."

Arturo rubbed his chin and looked from Estrella to Onofre. "Are you certain it's a good idea to build a seaport here in Rancho Ensenada? Once big cargo ships arrive, what will happen to the fishery? It might drive us out of business."

Onofre flashed a reassuring smile. "If we had a bigger port here, you'd have more markets and processing facilities. You'd have a hard time keeping up with the demand."

Estrella walked over to her father and put her arms around his shoulders. "Papá has a point, though. I think you should sell your boat to Banning and be happy with the money. Between the money you already have and the money he'd pay, I bet you'd be the richest man in Rancho Ensenada. I wouldn't dare serve you calabazas."

Onofre's gut churned. He needed to tell her how little money he actually had. "About that…"

Before he could speak, Luis knocked at the door. He came in waving an envelope. "My friend, a letter just came for you from Mr. Banning in Los Angeles." He thrust the letter into Onofre's face. "Open it. Read it!"

Onofre snatched the letter and read. A sense of relief washed over him. "It says, 'I'm intrigued by the prospect of investing in a way to repair ships without using a dry dock. Please come to Los Angeles at your earliest possible convenience so we may discuss this further.'"

"All right then," Estrella said, taking charge. "We'd better get busy assembling this boat. We can continue our discussion about an asking price while we work."

The next day they resumed working on the submarine boat. They loaded the engine along with pieces of the hull, linkages, rudder, and propeller onto Onofre's cart and transported it down to the beach. Estrella proved to be a good manager. She consulted with Onofre and Luis about the best people for given jobs and then put them to work.

The submarine took shape over the next week. It resembled an enclosed boat with a dome on top. The dome had windows so the pilot could look out and steer the ship. Windows also ringed the boat's bow. Monturiol's boat had been designed to scoop shellfish and coral into a basket. Onofre modified one arm so it had a simple two-fingered claw, while the other one held a cutter that could slice through rebar. If he succeeded in selling the idea to Banning, he could improve the arms so they would have greater range of motion and more tools, and reinforce them for greater strength. These first arms would suffice to demonstrate the concept.

At week's end, Onofre assembled a block-and-tackle rig and the team hauled the submarine out onto the pier and lowered it into the water.

"We should christen it," Luis suggested. "What are you going to name your creation?"

Onofre hadn't given much thought to a name. He'd been focused on lowering the ship's mass, while increasing its strength and propulsive force, so it would be better than Monturiol's submarine. The Spanish inventor had combined the Greek words for fish and boat, icthys and ploio, into *Ictíneo*. Onofre considered what the submarine boat represented to him personally. He saw more than a "fish boat." This new submarine represented his hopes and dreams for the future. He looked around at all the proud people gathered on the pier. This was no single man's dream. The village of Rancho Ensenada had come together to reach for the stars. He faced Estrella, whose name meant "star" and announced that he planned to name it after her. Estrella stepped forward, took Onofre's hands, and smiled.

The next morning, Onofre, Luis, Estrella, and Arturo met around the kitchen table in Arturo's small house. Estrella had fried corn tortillas and then smothered them in red chile for breakfast. Afterward, they pulled out a chart of the California coastline. Luis, Arturo, and Estrella spoke in low tones while Onofre made coffee.

"How fast do you reckon your submarine boat will go?" Arturo asked.

Onofre rubbed his chin. "Monturiol's submarine could travel at 4.5 knots on the surface. He had a larger crew and a smaller engine. I reckon we could make 6 knots in the *Estrella*."

Luis whistled. He exchanged a glance with Estrella, then took a measurement on the map. "By my estimate, it should take us just over a day to get to Los Angeles."

Onofre brought the pot over and poured coffee into cups. "Us?"

"We're coming with you," Estrella said, as though the decision should have been obvious.

Onofre set down the pot and held up his hands. "Whoa. Who said you were coming along? This is an untested craft. I don't want to risk you two on this journey."

Luis grabbed a coffee cup. "This isn't about what you want. You're an engineer, not a sailor. Los Angeles isn't that far away, but you still need help getting your boat there."

Onofre held out his hands. "All right, you can come." He turned to Estrella. "But you?"

"I know my way around boats, too, and you know I'm no damsel who needs a rescue."

Arturo chuckled. "It's true, I practically raised her on a boat."

"All right, all right." Onofre chuckled. "I can use the help, but pack your best clothes. We want to impress our big American investor."

Luis gave a sloppy salute. "Aye, aye, capitán!"

The next morning, Onofre, Estrella, and Luis discovered the team who'd assembled the submarine boat gathered on the pier to see them off. A mariachi band played a rousing selection of tunes, including the American sea tunes "Anchors Aweigh" and "Santiana." Onofre wondered how they'd all heard about the departure, then noticed Arturo smiling at them. Estrella went to him and gave him a kiss on the cheek and a long hug. Luis and Onofre each shook his hand. "We couldn't have done this without your help, Don Arturo."

"You take care of my daughter and my first mate," Arturo chided.

Onofre laughed and looked around at the smiling faces. They all hoped he would bring prosperity to their little town, which had fallen on hard times. He vowed not to let them down.

The crew loaded their luggage into the *Estrella*. Down inside the craft, Onofre opened the chemical valves. Within a few minutes, enough pressure had built in the boiler to get underway. Luis took the helm, which stood on an elevated platform so he could look out the windows in the bubble-shaped dome on top of the ship. Estrella stood below him at the chart table and kept a close eye on the compass while Onofre watched the engine's indicator dials.

Luis waved to the crowd as Onofre engaged the engine. The helmsman steered out into the Pacific Ocean's calm waters. Estrella kept him on a westward heading for the first part of the journey and traced how far they'd traveled based on the craft's speed.

Once they had made some progress and Onofre was satisfied the engine behaved as expected, he stepped forward and looked out through the view ports in the bow. The uppermost port was at the waterline, but the lower ports allowed a view of the fish below. Onofre delighted in the sights. As a mining engineer, this proved a new experience and the colorful undersea life captivated him. He suggested they try out the ship's capabilities and go for a short dive.

Conditions were nice enough that Estrella and Luis agreed. Onofre activated the ballast pumps and they dove about ten feet. Estrella joined Onofre by the front viewports. A school of gray fish with yellow tails swam by. A sea lion darted past the submarine scattering the fish. Estrella laughed and Onofre looked down into her eyes. "This is why I don't want to sell the boat. I want Mr. Banning to invest in it and in the town. Then we can do this more often."

She considered that for a moment. "Sometimes we have to give up what we think we want for what we actually need." For a moment, her eyes darted back toward Luis.

Just then, Luis, whose attention had been on the upper viewports, gasped. "Look out to starboard!"

Estrella and Onofre went to the boat's right-hand windows. A great white shark paralleled them, then shot forward, heading toward the sea lion. The mammal evaded the predator and soon both disappeared from view.

Estrella returned to the compass and took a measurement. "If we want to stay on schedule, we'd better surface again. Underwater viewing is fun, but it cuts our speed."

"And I'm getting a little light-headed here," Luis complained.

Onofre cursed himself and then opened the valve on the oxygen tank. Once air began to flow, he went to the ballast controls. He released the water and the boat rose to the surface where they continued on to the point where Estrella told Luis to steer northward.

They sailed through the day and into the night, taking turns sleeping on a bench mounted to the wall. Onofre had designed it as a place for people to sit, not really envisioning that people would make longer journeys in the submarine boat. If he built a version to explore the ocean, he'd need to make more provisions for passenger and crew comfort.

The *Estrella* arrived at the Port of Los Angeles in San Pedro Harbor just after noon. Luis scanned the docks for a likely place to tie up. He steered toward some fishing boats and brought the submarine up next to the pier. An old man came out of a shack and approached them. "There's a fee for tying up here at the port." He named a price in dollars.

"We only have pesos." Onofre pulled out some coins to show him. "But we're here at the invitation of Phineas Banning."

The dock worker narrowed his gaze.

Onofre retrieved the letter from his pocket and showed him.

The dock worker looked it over and finally nodded. "All right. Stay here. I'll get someone." He walked along the pier, past his shack, and then disappeared among some crates stacked on the shore, leaving Onofre, Luis, and Estrella to wonder whether or not he would return and what would happen when he did.

When he didn't return after a few minutes, Estrella retrieved a picnic basket from the boat and the three had lunch. Half an hour later, the old man returned followed by a man with thick sideburns, who wore a gray suit and blue waistcoat.

Onofre didn't know what Phineas Banning looked like, but suspected the new arrival was too young to be the investor. The man approached and held out his hand. "I'm Felix Anderson, one of Mr. Banning's clerks. I gather you have a project Mr. Banning might be interested in." Anderson's tone reminded Onofre of an adult patronizing a child.

"I wrote to Mr. Banning about my submarine boat." Onofre pointed to the wood and metal craft bobbing in the water below them.

Anderson sniffed. Onofre was glad he'd learned to speak English. He suspected this clerk would have dismissed him immediately if he used his native tongue. "People have built submarines before. Mostly they just kill the sailors unfortunate enough to crew them."

"We sailed here all the way from Rancho Ensenada," Luis chimed in, speaking heavily accented English. "We even tested it under water."

Anderson sniffed again.

Onofre's chest tightened and he had to suppress his disappointment that Banning had sent a clerk in his place. "Allow me to show you our boat and you can let Mr. Banning know whether it's worth his time."

Anderson made a show of considering the suggestion, then agreed to take a closer look at the submarine. Onofre pointed out the mechanical arms for work on ships. They clambered down onto the *Estrella* and entered through the hatch. The tour didn't take long. Anderson did study the engine carefully, though his expression remained neutral the whole time.

Once they finished the tour, they returned to the pier. Anderson made a few notes on a pad. "I can show you to a rooming house. I'll discuss what I've seen with Mr. Banning and let you know whether he'll meet with you by tomorrow morning."

"That's most kind." Onofre smiled.

Estrella and Luis exchanged sidelong glances.

Onofre spent a restless night tossing and turning. He'd left Luis and Estrella to find an inexpensive supper on their own. His stomach flip-flopped so much, he didn't think food would stay down and he wasn't certain he could afford to buy anything in the American town. He finally gave up on sleep when the morning sun's first rays shone in through his window.

He rose, dressed, and knocked on Estrella's door. When she didn't answer, he knocked again and listened. He couldn't even hear rustling sounds from within. He went next door and tried Luis's room. When Luis didn't answer, he tried the door. The room was empty and, as far as he could tell, no one had even slept in the bed. He feared Luis had found a watering hole that would take his pesos and he stayed up all night, drinking.

Swearing to himself he went downstairs where the landlord had provided a good breakfast. He ate and hoped Estrella or Luis would arrive. When he finished and they still hadn't turned up, he decided to go down to the pier and check on the submarine boat.

The moment he reached the wooden pier, he realized something was wrong. The mooring line had been replaced with a chain and the boat's hatch stood open. He ran along the pier and climbed inside. Two startled men looked up at him. "What are you doing?" he shouted.

"Mr. Anderson's orders," the taller man said. "We're here to remove the engine."

"This is my engine." Onofre grabbed a wrench and wielded it menacingly. "Now get out of here!"

The shorter man began rolling up his sleeves, but the taller one put his hand out. "We don't want any trouble. We'll get Mr. Anderson."

"You do that. I want to talk to him," Onofre growled.

The two men pushed past him and climbed out through the hatch. Onofre examined the engine. They'd only disconnected a couple of lines so far. They must have just started when he'd discovered them. Onofre set to work reconnecting the lines and considered the men. They apparently worked for Anderson. The clerk might be a lackey, but he hadn't seemed like a thief.

Onofre examined his work. Satisfied all had been restored to operation, he climbed out of the boat. On the pier, he discovered Estrella and Luis. They held hands and their faces revealed a mix of shame and defiance. Onofre looked from Luis to Estrella.

"What's going on here?"

Estrella squeezed Luis's hand, then released it and stepped forward. "Onofre. You've been so blind. I love you, but you've been so distant lately, obsessed with your boat. Luis has been there for me and he agrees with me that it's foolish to think Mr. Banning will invest in our quiet little harbor in México. The best deal we can make is selling the submarine and the engine. Mr. Banning's assistant was definitely interested."

She held out her hand and Onofre recoiled.

"The submarine boat is not yours to sell." Onofre's voice choked at the words.

"We all helped to build it, mi amigo," Luis said. "We weren't going to steal it. We'd share the profits with you, with the community."

Onofre clenched his fist. "The short-term profits from selling the submarine are nothing compared to what we could make if Banning invested in a company. Don't you see?" He couldn't stop tears from falling. "I spent all my money on the plans and parts to build this boat. I can't just sell it. I have to find a way to make a future with it."

Estrella couldn't meet his tear-filled eyes. "Luis told me. That's why we spoke to Anderson. Banning doesn't want to put money into México. If Banning doesn't, who will? Anderson said Banning's interested in the submarine. We negotiated a good price."

"You had no right to talk to Anderson without me. You didn't even give me a chance to make a case to him." Onofre stalked back to the submarine. "I'm going home now to find a way to make this work."

"How?" Luis pointed to the chain. "The boat's chained up. You aren't a sailor."

"No? You taught me how to pilot the boat on the way up." Onofre pointed to Estrella. "You told me how to read the charts." Onofre climbed through the hatch and closed it behind him. He opened the valves on the chemical supply, starting the reaction, then went forward and grabbed the mechanical arm controls. He swung the cutter arm around and extended it. He couldn't quite reach the chain. Using the grabber arm, he lifted the chain and pulled it toward the cutter. Just as he cut the chain, he noticed Estrella climbing through the hatch. He sighed as she entered.

She stepped forward and put her hand in the hidden pocket. For a moment, Onofre flinched, thinking she would pull out the gun and shoot him. Instead, she pulled out a calabaza – a squash – and placed it on the bench beside her, then stepped back. "I'm sorry, Señor Cisneros that I didn't have time to cook it, but I find you love this boat and you love Ensenada more than me."

Onofre took a deep shuddering breath. "I'm no one alone, mi corazón, but if I honored your deal with Anderson and Banning, I would be less than no one beneath your disregard."

She nodded, accepting his words, then climbed back through the hatch, closing it behind her. When she returned to the pier, Onofre saw the pressures had reached their nominal values. He engaged the drive, sailed a short distance, then dove under the water feeling very much alone.

Correspondence Transcribed in Code, Addressed to the Widowed Mrs. Clydebank

Beth Cato

February 22, 1880

Dearest Ma,

I am grateful that we foresaw the need for discreet correspondence so that I may share my true experiences with you, as I've been informed that the company does peek into employee mail under the assertion that they must guard trade secrets. I hope that you're not overly anxious as you await opportunities to get into town to fetch letters such as this. By the time you've begun to read these words, I pray you've already gotten my initial, rather bland, letters that were sent through normal means to the house. I know it will grate on your pride to pretend to others in town that I'm a simple secretary for the company, but at least you'll still be able to tell them I'm engaged in honorable work out in California.

First of all, let me assure you, my secret remains secure. My daily interactions with my male engineer colleagues are consistently respectful. My travel compartments were private, as are my quarters at the boarding house here in Hanford. I'm well aware of my constant need for vigilance, so pray do not spend the entirety of your next coded letter to me on preaching. I am attending church for that.

The airship journey west was a delight; I daresay, I was coddled in a way I heartily enjoyed. There are certainly perks to employment with the country's best manufacturer and purveyor of dirigible transportation! I oft worked on my blueprints while gazing out on the broad expanse of prairie and mountain below. That said, I am less pleased by my destination. I don't expect you would've heard of Hanford. Who would? It's a nascent farming town founded by the Southern Pacific. I didn't know this until I arrived, but my employer has purchased many California railways such as the Southern Pacific, just as they have around Arkansas. I'm nowhere near San Francisco and the company headquarters where we assumed I'd work. To my grief, I have yet to even see the ocean. I am posted inland, central within a place called the San Joaquin Valley. That second word is said as Wah-KEEN, almost like the word "walking."

This valley is massive, Ma, and I've seen little of it yet. The coastal hills, rounded and golden, are on clear days visible to the west, while to the east the Sierra Nevada Range is like a high-peaked wall. Much of my week here, however, we've been mired in what is called a "too-lee fog," the thickest fog I've seen in my life. But worry not—thus far I've only traveled within a few blocks of my boarding house. Once the fog lifts, I'll study the countryside for potential airship moorages. As I flew in, I could see sporadic farms spread throughout the area. My supervisors envision this place becoming one of the great bread baskets of the world, soon rivaling the Tigris and Euphrates of old, and the company will deliver those goods using their new line of airship freighters. Don't tell anyone this yet, not until you see mention in the papers, but these new ships will even be capable of flying across the Pacific with only a single stop in Hawaiian Territory. They can carry as much freight as the largest ocean vessel, but twice as fast.

I'm thrilled to be part of this innovation. I feel like I'm involved with something much bigger than myself, something important.

I cannot ignore that the pay is incredible as well. The first paycheck will address my loan to the school. My next earnings are yours, Ma, and do not faint when you open the envelope. I'll undo Pa's debts by the end of the year. I trust your judgment as to which bills to pay first, but do remember, the undertaker did not charge us as much as he ought to have when Pa died.

Some dollars anonymously sent his way will ease the burden of my inadequately-expressed gratitude.

I must end here, as my hand is cramping after a day's work atop this transcription into code.

Yours in truth,
El

———❁———

MARCH 3, 1880

Dearest Ma,

I had a close call today. My hand still trembles as I think of it. I've already shared what occurred with God, and as you are the only person upon this world I trust so, I now code this letter to you.

The fog has faded to a haze in recent days, and a work crew, as part of an experiment, was clearing reeds at the edge of a marsh. They were struggling, so I and the other engineers joined in the labor. As I moved my body, carrying loads and relishing in my strength, I felt the stitches of my chest binder tear. I knew that the clothes needed replacement, but I had never anticipated that the threads would fail in such a way — and me, a trained engineer! The look upon my face was surely peculiar, as one of my fellows asked after my wellbeing. I told him I'd pulled something in my back, and I used that as an excuse to hunch over as I withdrew from the company.

I felt ashamed that I couldn't help them as I ought, Ma, but also shame at how foolishly I almost revealed the truth of my sex. I delight in my born form, as you know, but even more, I crave to use my mind for science and mathematics. I will scorn skirts for all my years if it means I can be respected for the reliability of my numbers. All the better if I can keep you on the farm through my efforts.

I take up my pen some days later. My other letter with funds should've arrived at your house by now. I confess to the sin of pride, for I'm thrilled that I can take such a financial burden from your shoulders!

When I arrived here, I was embittered that I hadn't gotten to see the ocean—any ocean—yet, but I now find myself enthralled by the spring beauty of this valley, especially Tulare Lake.

This body of water is different than the lakes we know, Ma. I've been told that when the Sierras get little snow, the lake here in the valley will dry up, but in a moderately wet season such as this one, it's some seventy-five miles long and twenty-five miles in width, not deep, yet teeming with life. Mallards, coots, Canadian honkers—and so many more birds I cannot name! My peers could speak only of their desire to hunt. While I'm not one to shun a roast duck, I could only think that they were myopic. I knew you would've wept at the sight of these diverse piniioned beings. If only I had your gift with watercolors so that I might try to accurately capture the flutter of wings and the rippling reflections! I might give into the itch to sketch something, anyway, even if my effort will look like a child's work beside yours.

The sheer numbers of these birds do worry me, however, as they could create such profound hazards amid increased airship traffic. I will be making a deeper study of this matter.

Yesterday I rode out on my own south of Hanford so that I might take in the sights on my own time. The day was cool and fair, my spirit at ease. I returned to where we are preparing to erect a mooring mast at one of our sites (forgive me, I will explain more of this project on separate pages) and met a man there who was regarding the foundation with curiosity.

His questions verged on delicate company subjects. I redirected him as necessary. Well into our discussion, I mentioned my fondness of birds, at which point we began a horseback tour together as he named the flora and fauna. When he mentioned that he was a native, I asked if he'd been here since the Mexican land grant period, to which he said, with more good humor than I deserved, that his people had been here longer yet. He is of the native Tachi Yokuts.

I felt the fool, and I can imagine the chagrin with which you now regard me. Yes, yes, I should've known better than to make such an assumption based on his brown skin, having grown up with Cherokee people as my neighbors. And yet, since I've been here, no one has mentioned local Indians at all, as if they have ceased to be. I ruefully admitted to my ignorance. He informed me that the Yokuts are indeed greatly diminished these days. Tulare Lake, which he called Pa'ashi (I asked him how to spell it), was their source of nutritional and spiritual sustenance, in many ways, the center of their world, but they are not permitted to use it as they once did. Even more, its shores are dwindling as water is irrigated onto new farms. He fears that the lake will soon no longer exist, even during wet seasons.

I assured him that, while the company intends to utilize the land and ship its bounty elsewhere, I was part of a team present to ensure the job was done with efficiency and care. He was skeptical, observing that the company owns much of the local terrain and nearby railroads, and rules the air nationwide as well. Farmers in this area are irate, he said, because the company can charge what they like for the land, and people have to pay, leave, or suffice with leases. I confessed that, as a newcomer surrounded by company peers, I'd heard little of that perspective.

I left the conversation enlightened, but also somewhat disturbed. I have since taken notes on some of his bird identifications.

I must end here if I wish to mail this when I'm on an errand to Fresno tomorrow. Do not worry for me. I am doing good work here.

Yours truly,
El

ADDENDUM

Ma, pardon me for not including any drawings or schematics that would make this easier to comprehend, but I cannot blatantly share privy company details. Our code, at least, will greatly inconvenience anyone who seeks to spy on our correspondence.

My experience with the new line of airships is minimal, as my responsibility is to oversee the creation of the masts at which they'll dock.

And to answer the question that you ask on a regular basis, ground-landing airships are still in development, but I'm not hopeful of them being in commercial use in the next decade. Gravity and airships continue their contentious relationship.

Now, imagine the standard mooring mast that you might see in Springfield or Fayetteville. Black steel, like an oil derrick with exposed beams, but with stairs and a deck at the top to which an airship will be moored. You're used to seeing passenger vessels or perhaps small freighters, though I know the word "small" makes you laugh, as they are still huge compared to your usual horse and wagon. These new airships are fifty times as big. They can hold adequate wood and supplies to build and support a new town. Indeed, the shade cast by their massive envelopes could make sunflowers wilt.

A mooring mast to support such a ship must be massive in turn, as tall as a six-story building with a base almost as broad. It not only has several sets of stairs, but a freight lift large enough and strong enough to hoist a six-horse team with laden wagon or the equivalent.

I designed the mast that the company will use going forward, but my immediate issue is finding ground to support such a tower and the loads it must accommodate. As the Good Book tells us, we must build on the rock, not the sand. The San Joaquin Valley's east side tends to be marshy. The west side is too dry to support farms—cattle range there currently—and it is too far away to suit company needs. (I've also been told tarantulas are common there, which I shudder to consider.) We need to build masts in places that align with current ground transportation and civilization. Leveling the ground is the easy part; the earth must then evenly support the weight without sinking, whether the weather is wet or dry. This has proven more challenging than anticipated, for myself and the company, but science will prevail!

MARCH 30, 1880

Dearest Ma,

My recent letters to you, in straightforward English, were lies. Even though I understood the necessity of a pleasant front—even though I knew you understood it—I felt sick as I sent the envelopes.

My team's conclusions proved that most of the ground here, such as it is, cannot support the new airships. We're still going forward with the construction of one mast, however, and will test its capabilities in the coming months.

Even more, there's the issue of the birds, my beloved birds. I've told you more than once that my greatest concern in this business is a hydrogen fire within an airship envelope; currently, more than half of documented incidents were caused by bird strikes.

My notes for my superiors observed the increased risks of such high quantities of flocks, but with optimism. We can position masts to avoid nesting and congregation zones and take care with the times of day during which vessels are moored and unloaded. We can use scarecrows and glittery metal to discourage birds from certain areas, even as we maintain the wetlands. We can strive toward a balance with the natural terrain instead of playing arrogant despot.

The latter, sadly, is now their intent.

Ma, the goals they outline will aggressively expand and diversify their holdings. It's not enough that the company dominates the railroad and airship industry here, even as they are primary landowners; they are buying out small, local irrigation companies, and will expand that network broadly. They're recruiting experts who will design dams for the Sierras to restrain and regulate the flow of the melting snowpack and create deep new channels to bring water down to the valley. The Kings River, the greatest feeder for Tulare Lake, will be a controlled stream under their plan. They intend to eradicate the lake completely. The farmland beneath it is too rich. With the moisture depleted, masts will be able to stand, stabilized. Mosquitoes will not plague workers as they do now, creating widespread illness. The bulrushes, the waterfowl, even the frogs—they'll be gone as well.

I went for a ride to mull over the company's bulletin. While I was out, I came across the Tachi Yokut gentleman I spoke with some weeks ago. By necessity, I've become adept at presenting myself with the stoicism expected of a man, but I couldn't contain my emotions today. I said more than I ought to have about privy company news. He listened with compassion and concern, but then laughed in my face when I told him I was going to ask for permission to travel to San Francisco next week so that I might speak with the executive board myself. He told me they wouldn't see me past their dollar signs. I disagreed. I have more than enough evidence to convince them of the errors of their ways. The company prides itself on forecasting future needs and investments into the next decades. I can elucidate how they must look into the next century, and beyond. Resources are finite, and it's easy to forget that in times of plenty.

I didn't kindly part ways with my speaking companion this time. My inner turmoil transmuted into anger, and he was my target. His own ire rose. I suppose I'm fortunate that he wasn't the brash sort to pull a gun at the slightest provocation, but I still felt the sting of his parting vocabulary that consisted of "fool," "futility," and "vain effort."

I must do what's right. That is how you raised me.

Yours in truth,

El

April 5, 1880

Dear Ma,

By now I hope you received the postcard I sent from San Francisco. I have seen the Pacific Ocean and how it stretches to the ends of the earth, and such is the depth of my grief and shame.

I failed, Ma. I failed.

The company president himself was there on a visit to the western office. He and three other executives listened to my passionate plea. They looked at the schematics I presented to them of devices that could be used to discourage birds from gathering near masts, and how we can experiment with boring more deeply into the earth to stabilize our structures. They were quiet. Thoughtful. I believed I'd acquitted myself, and then the president spoke. He told me that if I wanted to preach, I should be in a church, not within the ranks of the company.

They didn't even bother to refute my data and schematics. The information simply doesn't matter. They are assured in their course and its profitability. Those are the numbers that matter to them, not the thousands upon thousands of birds they'll soon slaughter, some likely to extinction.

I was told to return to my work, and that out of respect for my "youthful passion," they'll leave no reprimand in my file. Yet word has spread, nevertheless. As I disembarked from the train in Hanford, one of my peers awaited me, calling out, "Elmore, the boss wishes to see you."

My superior's words flogged my soul. He'd hired me and complimented me to his superiors, he said, and in return, I'd shamed him.

In my room, I cried into my pillow so much, I later wrung water from the cloth.

To add salt to my wound, when I roused, I found a notice that my latest paycheck awaited me. Such a wealth of funds, such a blessing.

I must resume work now, even as I fight the urge to cry anew. Oh, Ma, what I'd give to feel your hug right now and not the vapors of your prayers, precious as they are!

El

APRIL 21, 1880

Ma,

How dare you reply, in one sentence telling me lightning struck the barn and burned it down, and in the next, you advise me to quit in good conscience. How can I do such a thing? The farm is almost debt-free! Nor is other work to my inclination. You say life will be easier if I can go by the name Eleanor again—truly? How can you say that, having endured what you've endured in your own life? If I donned skirts again, as a woman, I could only earn a pittance in a factory somewhere or engage in other drudgery far distant from my beloved numbers. How would that, as you say, be good for my soul? How?

I'm sorry. I've reread what I wrote hours later. You've told me, time and again, to release my burdens to you, that this is why we write in code. Even so, I thought we'd be using this script so that I could confess the difficulties of concealing my feminine form, not that I'd release my pent-up anger and frustration upon you.

The fact is that your letter shook me terribly. The loss of the barn is tragic enough, but you could've died. I want to take care of you, but I'm increasingly afraid that doing so means I can no longer take care of myself, body or soul. You tell me that money shouldn't decide all, that heaven is paved with gold, but we know what it's like to be unable to sleep because of hunger. I've loved my work here until now. Machinery is a delightful puzzle, and airships and their accoutrements are the best puzzles of all. But the company and their intents... I don't know, Ma. I don't know.

El

April 29, 1880

Ma,

My other letter to you, in plain English, states that a mast of my design is now officially under construction near Hanford. The pride I espoused was a lie. All I know is bitterness and shame. This mast is being built in a well-drained fringe of the lakebed, and will be debuted with great fanfare. The company will use the sheer size and scope of the mast to create excitement and speculation about the new airship line, as no information on that is public beyond the massive size of the construction hangars. The governor of California himself will attend the mast's debut, as will company executives. My boss has told me that I am not permitted to attend, even as I work the site each day. He doesn't want his superiors to see me and be reminded of my "transgression," even though this is utterly my creation. I couldn't conceal my anger from him.

Other people in the area are upset, too, as exorbitant prices have been posted for land now owned by the company. Gossip fuels rage that major investors from back east will be buying the land, and they'll lease out property at an increased rate. Some people here who've already created farms, as tenants of the company, will have the ground and their buildings sold out from underneath them. They get no payment for the improvements they made for the property, houses and barns included.

Have you seen anything about this injustice in the Arkansas papers, Ma? I doubt it. When I was back home, all I ever read about the company was that their technological innovations established them on the road of success, nothing about how the pavement of this thoroughfare was made of the shattered dreams of impoverished farmers and the bloodied white feathers of butchered egrets. I should also note that as the farmers here weep, I have yet to hear anyone consider who lived here first. The Yokuts are not mentioned at all.

I don't know what to do, Ma. I'm trying to keep food down, but the victuals provided by the company are lead in my gut. I am so lost. I'm praying for guidance. I don't know what else to do as the mast grows and grows as if it can reach heaven, while I feel like I'm the only one here who knows it truly extends toward hell.

Yours always,
El

MAY 8, 1880

Ma,

Forgive my brevity. I have found means to act. Do not believe what the papers say in the coming weeks. Do not believe other mail you may receive from the company. I'm taking precautions. Trust in the Lord. I will mail again when I can. Don't camp in town as you await word. Try to act as you would normally — and as part of that, retain your frugality. I do not know when or if I'll be able to send dollars your way again.

I'm following your advice, Ma. My soul is worth more than whatever the company pays me.

El

MAY 23, 1880

Ma,

The company has surely sent notice of my death by now. As this coded missive proves, I'm alive and well.

I will, with reason, omit many details, but I'll say that I've cast my lot with people who stand against the company. The man I've met in the past who showed me the birds — his inspections of our site were not out of mere curiosity. He sought to commit sabotage with the aid of other agents. His group is one of many around America and the world, because everywhere, there are places like Tulare Lake and people like the Tachi Yokuts who are diminished and forgotten.

I know the company and its projects with an intimacy few can rival. I know how to construct mooring masts and I also know how to bring them down.

The papers are saying that angry farmers destroyed the mooring mast with a bomb. I regret that they are being blamed, but I'm relieved that no arrests have been made. The Pinkertons on the case will need to concoct any evidence that is used against the farmers, as there is none.

I confess to you alone that my new companions wanted to bring down the mast with the executives and governor present. I refused to cooperate if such were their intentions. I will not save birds only to slay men. Instead, we timed it so that I was the only one present, conducting an inspection, when the blast occurred. My old boss has eulogized the slain Elmore Clydebank as a brilliant and devoted worker of the company, indeed, as a martyr. I cannot help but be amused.

Don't worry, Ma — I escaped the explosion with some temporary damage to my hearing and a few bruises. I'm fine. I am more than fine. My brain is alive with possibilities. I couldn't stop the company from within. Now, I will tap my knowledge as I take a different course.

My secret remains known only to you and God, and so it will stay. There are a few women among my current company, but as ever in this world, their roles are as restrictive as their corsets. I refuse to be bound by skirts or expectations.

I can hear the birds singing right now, Ma. These are not the birds of Tulare Lake, as I am now far from there, but I take comfort in their song because it is proof that they live. They live, and now I will do what I can to ensure that other birds continue to live as well.

Pray for me, as ever.
Yours truly,
El

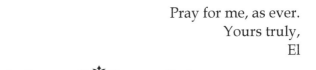

Author's Note: *The Mussel Slough Tragedy was a real shoot-out that occurred May 10, 1880 near Hanford, California, as angry farmers faced off against agents of the Southern Pacific Railroad; seven men died. I've tried to incorporate some facts about that event and the local environment, even as I created a distinctly alternate history steampunk take. After all, what is more 'punk' than rebelling against an all-powerful corporation? In reality, sadly, no one could truly stand up against the railroad or 'progress.' By the time I was born in Hanford a century after the Tragedy, Tulare Lake was something my grandparents spoke of with deep wistfulness. It is now a ghost that only returns in times of unusually heavy rain, such as the winter of 2022-2023. The Tachi Yokut Tribe celebrated and honored its return.*

THE MERRIE MONARCH'S MECHA

HILDY SILVERMAN

I CALLED THE HOUSEHOLD GUARD TO ATTENTION AS THE FOLDING STAIRS unfurled from the royal zeppelin, *Kaimiloa*. The sight of the massive, cigar-shaped airship juxtaposed against the sugar-white sands and rolling azure waves of the Pacific Ocean never failed to impress.

King David Kalākaua and his retinue descended moments later. The gathered crowd cheered his safe return, although my keen ears picked up more than a few jeers.

The king cut quite an impressive figure with his muttonchops and sweeping moustache. He wore a long leather greatcoat draped over a three-piece suit and medal-laden sash. He had spent nearly the entire year circumnavigating the globe in a highly ambitious endeavor that stirred excitement among his supporters. Among his detractors, he was gaining a reputation for spending too much of Hawai'i's funds on frivolous and self-aggrandizing pursuits.

What the latter failed to comprehend was that this audacious journey had been about more than becoming the first head of state to successfully travel around the world. It had been undertaken by the 'Merrie Monarch' (as several rivals dismissively referred to King Kalākaua) to visit leaders of states and commerce to solidify our kingdom's political sovereignty, import laborers for our sugar plantations, and establish new trade agreements.

I bowed low as King Kalākaua approached. "Captain Hiram Kahanawai," he acknowledged me with public formality. "A pleasure to see you again. I trust my dear Queen Kapi'olani managed well in my absence?"

"Yes, Your Majesty. She awaits your arrival at Iolani Palace. I understand a welcome home luau has been arranged."

The king grinned broadly beneath his thick, upwardly curled moustache. "I have no doubt the queen felt compelled to oversee every detail." He rubbed his ample belly. "As much as I enjoyed the exotic cuisines sampled during my travels, I have missed the delights of home."

I signaled my men to escort King Kalākaua and his staff to the waiting steam engine. We cleared the path of supporters waving leis and protestors shaking fists. After we'd climbed into the blond koa wood and brass-trimmed passenger car, Kalākaua dropped all formality, indicating I should take the cushioned seat directly across from him.

"Hiram, my boy, I have so much to tell you!" His dark brown eyes veritably glowed with an internal flame. "I have met with some of the greatest minds. Of course, there were some disappointments… that deranged fellow in Menlo Park with his unworkable concepts. But then there was Mr. Tesla and his remarkable creations. Gaslights? The past! We shall install his marvelous coils at Iolani and enjoy consistent and efficient lighting. My palace will outshine even the United Americas' White Palace! Can you imagine?"

I smiled, drawn in by his enthusiasm. "It sounds amazing." *And expensive*. I kept that concern to myself.

"I have already asked Gibs to allocate the funds to the Lodge," the king said, as if reading my mind. "Fifty-thousand or so should be sufficient."

I made a mental note to increase patrols. This enterprise would likely go over like a leaden zeppelin once word got out—which it inevitably would.

Gibs, as Kalākaua so casually referred to him, was Walter Murray Gibson, the kingdom's finance minister, a man of—to be polite—colorful background. Gibson was likely to be named Prime Minister now that Kalākaua had returned. Given that he was not a native Hawaiian (born in Britain, raised in the United Americas) and that his qualifications consisted of adventuring, leading religious fanatics (until he was excommunicated for his extremism), gunrunning, and embezzling, precious little recommended him for such a prestigious government role. However, he had endeared himself to the king over the years, supporting Kalākaua's lifelong devotion to Hawaiian independence, even as pressure from annexationists within, and the neighboring U.A. without, increased. Rumor had it that Gibson was whispering in Kalākaua's ear that he should pursue an empire of his own.

Kalākaua shrugged off his greatcoat. "This served me well while sailing the frigid air currents." He handed it to a valet, who folded it neatly over his forearm and departed with a bow. "Quite unnecessary back in the warm embrace of Oahu. A pity—it billows so impressively when I walk. Did you notice?"

"Indeed, Your Majesty. Quite impressive… billowing."

"It is also high time work on the *Kamehameha I* got underway. Ten… no, twelve feet tall. More, perhaps? I want the ground to tremble when he marches." He tugged the waxed tips of his mustache in contemplation. "I shall consult PoKo."

My thoughts strayed to Po'omaikelani, or PoKo, the endearment only those closest to her were permitted to use. Second sister of Queen Kapi'olani, she was the Chief Engineer overseeing numerous projects for the crown. This included all work done within Iolani Palace by Kalākaua's Freemason Lodge, Le Progres de L'Oceanie, making sure they remained focused and on-budget per her sister's directive. While Queen Kapi'olani adored Kalākaua, she was well aware of his tendency to ignore financial restrictions on his ambitious conceits.

I envisioned PoKo's eyes darkening like skies presaging a typhoon when her brother-in-law informed her of the changes he intended. The palace's reconstruction had only just been completed; quite necessary since it had become rundown by the end of the Kamehameha dynasty. Now she would not only have to upgrade the lighting, but simultaneously undertake construction of an automaton which, as the Merrie Monarch grew more excited by his own words, kept growing to outlandish heights.

I made a mental note to secure an extra bottle of okolehao before visiting PoKo next.

Six Months Later

PoKo crawled out of the automaton's stomach and climbed down a ladder. She wiped grease on her leather apron, managing a sincere, if weary, smile before we touched foreheads and exchanged breath.

"Dare I ask?" I shifted my gaze reluctantly from her face to her enormous creation. Her handpicked team of engineers, mechanics, and metal workers toiled along its legs, which were nearly twice the height of an average man. The midsection to which they were joined gaped widely to reveal its inner workings — pistons, gears, struts, and less easily identifiable components.

"We are somewhat behind schedule." PoKo sounded like she had just confessed to an affair. For a woman of such organization and focus, a slip in her planned timetable was nearly as humiliating. "We've run into some challenges with the autonomic synaptic functions." She gestured to the two halves of a giant head in the midst of the enormous palm-thatched workshop and launched into a detailed rundown of issues.

I understood only bits and pieces like *gear drives* and *Lovelace computations* and *backup piloting*. Other men might become irritated by a woman speaking so far above his ability to comprehend, but to me, the brilliance of PoKo's mind only made her more attractive. It was why I fell so fast for her back when we were among the students selected to be sent to the United Kingdom by King Kalākaua. Those years abroad gave us quite some time to become well-acquainted, despite our enrollments in separate schools — mine Sandhurst Academy for military science; hers Brunel Institute for mechanical engineering and design.

PoKo abruptly jabbed the center of my chest. "I've told you to stop me when I ramble! Instead, you stand there grinning at my litany of woes."

I chuckled and patted her shoulders. "How am I to learn if I don't listen?"

"You hardly need to understand the intricacies of automaton construction in your role, captain."

I brushed a stray black curl from her forehead. "Perhaps not, but I do need to understand whatever is most important to you, ku'ualoha."

PoKo's smile promised more than mere words could convey. But then she returned to business. "At least Iolani is finally complete… until David meets *another* great inventor and decides it must be upgraded again." She referred to the king by his Anglicized name — which he typically eschewed — with the casualness only family could. "Have you heard the latest? Ol' *Gibs* has convinced him that it's time for a formal coronation."

I nodded and frowned. "I am aware. I still do not understand the rationale, especially given the king's increasing… concerns."

Kalākaua had developed a fear of assassination, and it was growing proportionately to rising public disapproval of his schemes. His multiple Iolani Palace projects were deeply unpopular. Many viewed it as yet another example of Kalākaua being a self-indulgent spendthrift.

Separately, the concept of a Pacific Empire thrilled many but worried others, given the power it would convey to an Emperor Kalākaua. Our people had only to cast their gaze toward the U.A. to observe the dangers of unchecked power.

Kalākaua's steadfast refusal to sign over our islands certainly chafed the U.A.'s current monarch, Chester Arthur. As a mollifying gesture, Kalākaua planned to re-sign the lease for use of Pearl Harbor by their naval and airship forces; a move to which Prime Minister Gibson strenuously objected. This disagreement followed Gibson's diplomatic junket to Japan, from which he returned in the company of an ambassador, Mr. Taro Ando. It was the only advice of his I could recall Kalākaua rejecting and it remained a sore subject between them.

"This is why I am under such pressure," PoKo was saying. "My timeline for completion of the *Kamehameha I* keeps shrinking. It is meant to be tested and fully functional to lead the coronation procession."

I looked across the workshop at huge bronze arms resting on their sides. An engineer manipulated rods within the shoulder of one while another observed the fingers for movement, scowled at the lack thereof.

"Despite David's… paranoia, reasonable concerns, call them what you will, he is keen on Gibson's concept," PoKo said. "Since his first crowning was so rushed, due to the precarious situation at the time, I suppose I understand why."

I remembered that dark time all too well. The Emmaites, rabid supporters of Queen Emma, had rioted when she lost the election. Even some members of the Guard at the time had sided against Kalākaua, all of whom had been dealt with severely once the riots were put down.

"Now this makes more sense." I nodded toward the half-constructed automaton. "It will not only honor the great Kamehameha I, it will associate Kalākaua with him as his rightful heir. Still, given the current climate?"

"It is my duty to obey my brother-in-law's directives, not analyze them." PoKo made a shooing motion with both hands. "Stop distracting me. I have an ungodly amount of work to do in an equally unholy amount of time. Aloha, ku'ualoha."

I was summoned to the palace and told to wait outside the Blue Room. Although I did not intend to eavesdrop like a nosy housemaid, the doors had been left ajar and the room's acoustics magnified speech. I caught the end of a conversation between Kalākaua, Gibson, and Ambassador Ando.

"…them from leveraging Pearl Harbor to strike at the heart of your nascent empire!" Ando was insisting.

"Nonsense," Kalākaua huffed. "Do you truly believe the United Americas are so fearful of their Pacific neighbors they would do such a thing?"

"You have no idea what they are capable of, Your Majesty." Ando's tone held menace.

"Given the credible threats against Your Majesty's life," Gibson interjected, "I believe our esteemed visitor is correct. An empire will be far more difficult to annex, which is surely the Americas' ultimate goal. Ridding ourselves of the most viable threat to your well-being, not to mention Hawai'i's, makes sense."

"The U.A. is insatiable, King Kalākaua," Ando said. "Pearl Harbor will become a base of operations for crushing Hawaiian independence and sweeping her remains under their eagle's wing. I implore you to reconsider."

Kalākaua snapped, "My decision is final. The new lease has already been drawn up and sent to King Arthur for signature. It would be a diplomatic insult to renegotiate now."

Awkward farewells followed. I stepped aside just in time to avoid being trampled by the hastily exiting Ando, Gibson at his heels looking like a pup desperate to make amends for piddling on his master's shoe. Neither spared me a glance.

"Come in, Captain," called Kalākaua.

I entered the Blue Room, so called for its blue décor, including a collection of velvet upholstered chairs set around the perimeter and long velvet drapes pulled back with gold ropes. Kalākaua indicated that I should close the doors behind me, which I did before approaching the wide, cushioned chair on which he sat. "I trust you heard at least part of that?"

I knew better than to prevaricate—and clearly had no need to, as I realized the king had deliberately left the doors open and scheduled my arrival purposefully. "This explains why the Prime Minister objects to the Pearl Harbor lease." I took care to keep my tone neutral. "The ambassador has his ear."

"Or some other body part." Kalakaua muttered. "Thick as thieves, those two."

"But why should Japan care? It doesn't affect them."

"Gibs knows my position on Hawai'i's independence remains firm as ever." Kalākaua twisted the tip of his moustache around his forefinger. "We also agree that our future would be best served by uniting the Pacific Isles into a singular empire... as does Japan, it seems. Not that they *should* fear it. I am not so foolish as to seek world domination."

"I doubt Japan fears conquest," I agreed. "Their technology is rumored to surpass what the rest of the world has even imagined, let alone possesses."

"Speaking of which, the ambassador gifted me this as a gesture of goodwill," Kalākaua indicated the gold-trimmed porcelain pot and matching teacups set atop the tea table between us, "along with a lovely jasmine tea from his homeland." He depressed a jewel set into the teapot's lid. A soft hiss was followed by a waft of steam from the spout. "A self-heating pot—quite marvelous! Shall we indulge?"

I poured for us and took a sip. The tea was a touch bitter for my taste. Kalākaua merely sniffed his before setting the cup down and launching into a litany of concerns regarding security for the upcoming coronation. I reassured him that the Household Guard had thoroughly surveilled the gardens in which the public ceremonies were to be held and prepared myriad defenses to keep everyone safe.

He nodded approval. "You are, of course, familiar with our dear PoKo's work?" A gleam in his eye accompanied the inquiry.

Warmth suffused my face. The king was well aware of my relationship with his sister-in-law, and though he heartily approved, he also enjoyed watching me squirm whenever the subject arose.

I cleared a tickling in my throat. "The *Kamehameha I* automaton is nearly complete."

"Excellent." The mirth left his face. "You think it foolish, don't you? Like everyone else."

I nearly choked and set down my half-empty cup. "Your Majesty, I would never presume..."

"I am not cross with you, or even those who criticize my every ambition." He sighed wearily. "I know my reputation. People simply do not understand the importance of appearances when it comes to presenting Hawai'i as a leader in modernization and worthy of respect by other nations. Nevertheless," he drummed his fingers against the gilded armrest, "utilizing the automaton for mere spectacle might be... short-sighted."

My stomach roiled. After all the money, time, and effort invested in the automaton, was Kalākaua about to call the project to a halt?

He continued, mercifully unaware of my discomfiture. "It is capable of so much *more*. With a few adjustments, it could offer protection beyond human ability."

"Y... you mean to weaponize the automaton?" I swallowed with difficulty, my mouth and throat somehow drier than before the tea. "Have you lost faith in the Household Guard? Do you doubt *me*?"

"Of course not." Kalākaua shook his head vigorously. "I know your men will do their utmost. However, a fully equipped automaton could increase your defenses. Its sheer size alone, combined with weaponry augmentations? It would give you superior firepower to take on... Hiram? Is something wrong?"

I was swaying. Heat and ice coursed through me in alternating waves. The muscles in my throat and chest contracted until I could scarcely draw breath. I scrabbled to open the high collar of my uniform, hands shaking too violently to control.

As if through an elongating tunnel, I saw Kalākaua reaching for me. "Steady on, I've got...."

The rest his words were lost as I pitched forward into darkness.

There was no doubt I had been poisoned. It was equally certain I had not been the intended victim.

PoKo was by my side when I first opened my eyes in the infirmary. She squeezed my hand and exclaimed, "Ku'ualoha! I never lost faith you would return to us." Tears streaked her cheeks, eyes red and swollen.

I longed to wrap my arms around her, but they seemed as detached as the arms of the automaton had been. I struggled to speak, to comfort her with words if not touch, but only managed a low moan.

"Shh, it's all right. The physics are still clearing the poison from your system." She nodded to indicate a bottle hanging from a hook. Viscous fluid dripped through a thin tube ending in a small needle inserted into the back of my hand. "Improvement may be slow, but you *shall* recover."

One of my lieutenants informed me later that Ando and Gibson had vanished. This despite the Guard having been immediately deployed by a suspicious King Kalākaua following my collapse.

During the long weeks that followed, I slowly regained some ability to speak. I recovered enough control of my body to tend to daily hygiene. But my muscles remained weak. My hands trembled almost constantly. I began to despair of ever being restored to the robust condition I had previously taken for granted.

King Kalakaua refused my proffered resignation, stating that I could still direct the Guard from the windup chair I now required to get around. His expression when he told me this was guilt-ridden, undeservedly so.

Only two bastards were to blame.

Knowing *who* had poisoned me offered scant comfort. I wanted to know *why*. What prompted an ambassador, who had previously announced his country's eagerness to establish a consulate and friendly relations, to turn assassin? All I kept coming back to was the Pearl Harbor arrangement. But then what was Gibson's motive for abandoning his high position and the promise of even greater power should Kalākaua become an emperor? What could he have hoped to gain by convincing the king not to re-sign... or by killing him to guarantee he didn't?

The coronation day arrived and I still had no answers. Meanwhile, the signed Pearl Harbor lease was delivered, and King Kalākaua declared he would co-sign it after the ceremony.

I wound my chair using the large key in the back and rode to PoKo's workshop, as I had been doing regularly since leaving my infirmary bed. If a second assassination were planned, it would most likely be attempted that day. We had to be prepared.

"Is it ready?" I called up to PoKo.

She climbed down the ladder, having adjusted the large doors set into the breast of the now-completed *Kamehameha I.* "It won't work!" Her tone was despairing. "The repeating rifle barrels in the fingertips won't extrude and retract reliably. Plus, the Lovelace Brain cannot operate the other augmentations... there simply wasn't enough time to reconfigure."

She nearly tore her hair free of the pearl diadem around which it was carefully woven. "David will be *furious*, not to mention terrified, without his mighty guardian leading the procession." She began pacing, muttering, "Must give up on wholly autonomous function. Switch to pilot mode… manual operation…"

"Wait, what?" I had observed while PoKo and her team put the finishing touches on the bronze-plated colossus, and so was aware of the pilot's compartment. "I thought manual piloting was for testing purposes only."

"Correct," said PoKo. "A pilot changes the dynamic… the automaton is reduced to a mecha. But better to depend upon a functioning human brain than an incomplete artificial one. But who shall—"

"Me."

PoKo gawped. "What?"

I pushed against the armrests and stood, legs trembling as they reluctantly accepted my weight. "Who is better qualified? An engineer cannot recognize subtle indicators of an impending attack. I possess the necessary weapons training. I should be the one to pilot the automa… the mecha."

"No, Hiram, that is… *auwe!*" She buried her face in her work-gloved hands. When she looked up again, it was streaked with mingled grease and tears. "I know you're right, but," her voice broke, "I so very nearly *lost* you."

I squeezed her shoulders. "That marvelous creation of yours shall encase me securely within millimeters-thick bronze. I need to be on the field, to protect my king and his family. *You*. Please, I must be… vital again."

PoKo chewed her lower lip. She nodded and led me to the mecha. "Lower it," she ordered. "Then unlock the pilot's compartment."

The *Kamehameha I* knelt, gears in its massive knees whirring loudly. I heard clicking sounds as locks released along the barely visible seam running down its center. Doors swung open to reveal a small chair and just enough space to sit. With PoKo's assistance, I awkwardly climbed into the cramped section and found myself surrounded by pulleys, levers, buttons, and a periscope.

"Everything is labeled. See the placards here, here, and here." PoKo pointed to engraved brass plates beneath each control. She peeled back the glove covering her left wrist and consulted a strapped chronometer. "We have scant time to review what each does and proper operation."

"Then it is fortunate I have been observant these past months." I hoped my tone was as reassuring as intended.

Encased in the mecha, I stood at the edge of the gardens watching the final preparations for the procession. I was amazed by everything the sensory tubes conveyed — scents of plumeria, hibiscus, and gardenia; strands of music from a small orchestra rehearsing across the wide lawn. The periscope leading to Kamehameha I's eyes included magnifying lenses I could swap between at the turn of a dial, enabling me to see much farther than the human eye.

A trumpet sounded. Two Guardsmen opened the iron gates set into the stone walls surrounding the gardens to admit guests. I glanced behind as the royal family, led by the king and queen, lined up for the formal march. The Household Guard took up positions along their flanks and rear as the opening strands of *Hawai'i Pono'ī* sounded. King Kalākaua nodded up to me and I shifted levers to make the mecha nod in return.

The procession began.

I admit to making a few minor errors initially. Nothing fatal, but the mecha did flatten a lovely Bougainvillea. However, I soon had *Kamehameha I* confidently marching along in time to our national anthem. The guests standing along the parade route gasped and cheered.

We stopped just before the gazebo under which Kalākaua would be formally crowned. He climbed to the podium within and raised a voice-amplifying speaking tube to address the crowd, as family and courtiers arranged themselves behind him. I tore my gaze from PoKo, who looked every inch the resplendent princess in her floral silk gown (and without a trace of grease remaining to mar her complexion) to continue surveilling for threats.

A distant gleam caught my attention. Whatever caused it was shrouded by a thick copse of banyan trees. Shifting lenses brought into focus something wholly at odds with its surroundings: a pagoda, smaller than the norm for those structures. More concerning, it had seemingly come into existence within the hour, as otherwise my Guards would have spotted it during one of their earlier patrols of the untamed woods beyond the palace gardens.

Increasing magnification revealed the gleam's source — the lens of a scope mounted atop a dark object jutting from the second eave of the three-tiered structure. The muzzle of some form of cannon spat phosphor, a bright green glow that nearly blinded me as it arched through the sky toward the gardens.

I activated the mecha's voice box and boomed, "Everyone down now!"

Attendees dove for cover. Guardsmen pulled the royal family down and shielded them bodily. I bent the mecha over the gazebo and those within. Something slammed into its back with such force I had to shift levers to brace its limbs, lest it crush the very people I meant to protect. The bronze casing heated, leaving me soaked in perspiration and wheezing hot air.

Kamehameha I held, and after several fraught moments, the heat dissipated. I asked, "Is everyone all right?"

My men rose and Kalākaua waved to indicate all were well. Relieved, I ordered one contingent of the Guard, "Get everyone into the palace now and raise all door and window shields!" To another, I said, "See to crowd control and clear the gardens."

I knew the would-be assassin was not done. Judging by the amazing distance his projectile had traveled, I feared he might be capable of firing upon Iolani itself. *Might he breach its shields? Knock down the walls entirely?*

I brought the mecha back to its feet and tried extruding the repeating rifles from its fingertips. Only a grinding sound resulted.

Frustrated, I shifted the mecha into highest gear, stepped over the stone fence, and headed for the mysterious pagoda. I had no way of knowing how long it would take the assassin—Ando, I assumed—to reload and fire again. However, I had begun a countdown after the first blast for future assessment.

My lenses remained focused on the cannon-like weapon, cursing that *Kamehameha I* could not actually run. At best, it managed a jolting momentum that bounced me in my seat most uncomfortably.

The canon muzzle glowed green again. My heart beat a rapid tattoo and my muscles clenched with dread. Instinctively, I crossed the mecha's thick arms in front of my compartment and lowered its head.

I didn't see a physical projectile, but some energetic force struck the arms hard enough to nearly topple *Kamehameha I*. Crackling static echoed within. Green lightning bolts coursed down the bronze exterior, then deflected onto nearby trees and brush, which burst into flame. The concussive force tossed me like a macadamia shaken in its shell. I inadvertently struck a lever that caused the mecha to fling its arms wide, smashing two burning trees to the sward.

Quickly as possible, I righted the mecha and made its feet stomp and hands bat out the fires whilst estimating thirty seconds remained before the next blast. Hoping no embers reignited in my wake, I re-engaged forward momentum, elongating the mecha's stride until it all but leapt through the trees and over obstructions.

I reached the pagoda just as a faint green glow began swirling within the muzzle. I drew back the mecha's arm, clenched its fingers, and swung.

The enormous fist slammed into the cannon, crumpling it like origami. The nascent charge could find no release through the now-crushed muzzle. A screech heralded that it was too late for the assassin to abort firing.

I dropped *Kamehameha I* to its knees just as the cannon exploded.

A cloud of bright green phosphorescence swirled and dissipated around the top half of the pagoda, which was blown into matchsticks that rained down several moments later. My ears rang as the cacophony echoed through the hearing apparatus before I was able to switch it off.

I ran a cursory system check and discovered that, while the shell of *Kamehameha I* was now covered in dents and scorch marks, it remained functionally intact. I spent the next several minutes beating out burning detritus and smothering small flames along the trunks of the baobabs. Fortunately, the worst of the blast had been directed skyward.

A figure stumbled forth from the torn screen of the pagoda's bottom tier. Gibson looked quite the worse for wear, face battered and blood-streaked, his usually pristine suit torn and filthy.

"Halt!" I boomed, cranking the voice box louder than necessary given he was right below me. Petty, perhaps, but I found it gratifying to watch him clutch his ears and nearly tumble onto his ass. "Walter Gibson, you are under arrest for high treason!"

His mouth worked a few moments before he managed to shout, "Is... is that you, Captain Kahanawai? Oh, thank God, I was given to understand you were hopelessly crippled!"

It took all my self-control not to stamp him out like another stray ember. I lowered to one knee and glared through the periscope. "No thanks to you and your venomous co-conspirator! How *dare* you try to murder our king, you worthless ingrate! King Kalākaua will have you hanged for trying to poison him and endangering his entire—"

"Wait!" Gibson waved his arms, eyes round with fright. "Captain, you misapprehend!" He yanked up his sleeves and revealed ligature marks around each wrist. "It was all Ando, I swear it! He never said a word about poisoning Kalākaua or harming him in any way. I *never* would have… in fact, as soon as I heard about you, I told him I was finished. I would have nothing more to do… but then he said I knew too much. He's held me within his confounded apparatus for weeks!"

He shook his head. "I don't know why he didn't just kill me… kept prattling on about future need, my role in what was to come. A madman, I tell you… completely insane!"

Unimpressed, but bound to learn all there was to know about this conspiracy, I said, "You *will* tell us everything, and just maybe the king will permit you to continue drawing breath in prison. But first, where is Ando?"

Gibson flung his arms wide. "I assume scattered all around us. He had to reload and fire his phosphorous cannon manually."

I wrapped the mecha's hands around Gibson, lifted him bodily as it stood. Unwilling to accept his word if he stated the sky was blue, I examined the crumpled remains of the pagoda. I discovered naught but an interior filled with the smoking remains of technology I could not identify. Scans of our surroundings revealed no traces of Ando either.

I carried my squirming prisoner back toward Iolani Palace to face a full inquiry — and the king's justice.

Gibson confessed from his prison cell to having entered into (what he thought) would be a mutually beneficial relationship with the self-proclaimed ambassador: once Ando became Chief Consul of a new Hawaiian consulate, he would leverage his role to convince our neighbors, including the powerful Samoa, to join the proposed Pacific Empire with enticements of technology and other enrichments from Japan. To Gibson, it had seemed an expedient way to bring his and Kalākaua's vision of a united Pacific to fruition.

In exchange, Ando demanded that Gibson convince the king not to lease Pearl Harbor to the United Americas, and eventually sever all ties with the mainlanders. "He claimed to possess a means to travel through dimensional cracks and visit not only our future, but the futures of realms parallel to ours."

"Outlandish," Kalākaua scoffed. He stroked his mustache. "Might it be possible?"

"I doubted as well, Your Majesty," said Gibson. "However, Ando insisted he had visited myriad versions of Japan's future, witnessing common events that included a great war they would lose because the U.A. entered the fray. The result was always disastrous for Japan — either outright destruction of their empire, or at minimum, a significant loss of power."

That was worrisome. What if Japan sent more assassins? "Did he inform his government? His emperor?"

Gibson shrugged. "He claims he tried but was not believed. Their emperors are considered infallible, which rendered his suggestion of one engaging in an unwinnable war akin to saying God would fall before Satan — blasphemy to even propose. Ando was dismissed as a crackpot of Edison's proportions, relieved of his status and honor as an inventor. A most horrible fate in their society."

"And his claims of being an ambassador?" Kalākaua prompted.

"Prevarication. I do not know what he did with their real ambassador, but Ando took his place with the goal of eliminating your Pearl Harbor arrangement. Apparently in every future, an attack on that base convinces the U.A. to destroy the Japanese Empire." Gibson shuddered. "He described witnessing the Americas unleash an inconceivably evil weapon... giant mushroom-shaped clouds, instantaneous vaporization, destruction on an unimaginable scale. That vision tormented Ando's every waking moment."

"How dismaying for him." I could muster little sympathy for the man who had tried to kill my king, upended my life, and endangered my beloved to boot. "So that justified assassination?"

"That was *his* idea!" Gibson gripped the bars of his cell. "I swear on all that is holy, I would *never* have agreed to such a thing. I had no idea that tea was poisoned or that Ando would leap from diplomacy to regicide in the same afternoon." His shoulders slumped. "I failed to realize just how deranged he was until it was nearly a fait accompli."

Kalākaua and I exchanged looks. I sensed Gibson, for all that he was an opportunist and a fool, told the truth. From the king's expression, he concurred.

So, it was prison for Gibson rather than the noose. The Japanese were informed of the faux ambassador's plot, which they responded to with appropriate dismay. They profusely apologized and offered to discuss opening a consulate in earnest, as a gesture of goodwill.

Members of the Household Guard were deployed to retrieve the pagoda, only to discover its ruins had utterly vanished. This disappointed Kalākaua greatly, as he'd wanted its workings studied to learn whatever secrets lay within. Where it disappeared to, and how, were mysteries that remained unsolved.

I eventually recovered to where I could walk with a cane and my tremors only occurred when fatigued. The king, in his gratitude, named me the official pilot of his mecha alongside my captaincy. "This way, you may remain my strong right hand," he proffered.

My stunned reaction to this gracious gesture made PoKo laugh. "A simple thank you will suffice, ku'ualoha. Besides," she added coyly, "I am told we might consider the mecha an engagement gift… assuming the roles of pilot *and* husband are acceptable?"

I bowed to Kalākaua, took PoKo's hand, and kissed the back of it as I had witnessed gentlemen in the United Kingdom do during sojourn there. "King Kalākaua, Princess Po'omaikelani," I said, grinning, "Both would be my profound honor."

About the Authors

Cynthia Radthorne is an author and illustrator residing in the Pacific Northwest. Her characters, both honorable and devious, populate her series of Asian-themed fantasy novels, The Tales of Tonogato. Her illustrations have appeared on book covers, web sites, trading card games, and at art show displays at science fiction and fantasy conventions. At Cynthia's website, www.CynthiaRadthorne.com, one can peruse a sample from one of her books and view her art gallery.

Aaron Rosenberg is the best-selling, award-winning author of over fifty novels, including the DuckBob SF comedy series, the Relicant Chronicles epic fantasy series, the Areyat Islands fantasy pirate mystery series, the Yeti urban fantasy series, the *Dread Remora* space-opera series, and, with David Niall Wilson, the *O.C.L.T.* occult thriller series. His tie-in work contains novels for *Star Trek, Warhammer, World of WarCraft, Stargate: Atlantis, Shadowrun, Mutants & Masterminds*, and *Eureka and short stories for The X-Files, World of Darkness, Crusader Kings II, Deadlands, Master of Orion, and Europa Universalis IV*. He has written children's books (including the original series STEM Squad and Pete and Penny's Pizza Puzzles, the award-winning *Bandslam: The Junior Novel* and the #1 best-selling *42: The Jackie Robinson Story*), educational books on a variety of topics, and over 70 roleplaying games (including the original games *Asylum, Spookshow*, and *Chosen*, work for White Wolf, Wizards of the Coast, Fantasy Flight, Pinnacle, and many others, the Origins Award-winning *Gamemastering Secrets*, and the Gold ENnie-winning *Lure of the Lich Lord*). He is a founding member of Crazy 8 Press.

Aaron lives in New York with his family. You can follow him online at gryphonrose.com, on Facebook at facebook.com/gryphonrose, and on Twitter @gryphonrose.

Jeff Young is a bookseller first and a writer second—although he wouldn't mind a reversal of fortune.

He is an award-winning author who has contributed to the anthologies: *Afterpunk, In an Iron Cage: The Magic of Steampunk, Clockwork Chaos, Gaslight and Grimm, Phantasmical Contraptions and other Errors, By Any Means, Best Laid Plans, Dogs of War, Man and Machine, If We Had Known, Fantastic Futures 13, The Society for the Preservation of C.J. Henderson, Eccentric Orbits 2 & 3, Writers of the Future V.26, TV Gods and TV Gods: Summer Programming.* Jeff's own fiction is collected in *Spirit Seeker, Written in Light* and TOI *Special Edition 2 – Diversiforms.* He has also edited the *Drunken Comic Book Monkey* line, *TV Gods* and *TV Gods –Summer Programming* and is the managing editor for the magazine, *Mendie the Post-Apocalyptic Flower Scout.* He has led the Watch the Skies SF&F Discussion Group of Camp Hill and Harrisburg for twenty-two years. Jeff is also the proprietor of Helm Haven, the online Etsy and Ebay shops, costuming resources for Renaissance and Steampunk.

James Chambers received the Bram Stoker Award® for the graphic novel, *Kolchak the Night Stalker: The Forgotten Lore of Edgar Allan Poe* and is a four-time Bram Stoker Award nominee. He is the author of the short story collections *On the Night Border* and *On the Hierophant Road*, which received a starred review from *Booklist*, which called it "…satisfyingly unsettling"; and the novella collection, *The Engines of Sacrifice*, described as "…chillingly evocative…" in a *Publisher's Weekly* starred review. He has written the novellas, *Three Chords of Chaos, Kolchak and the Night Stalkers: The Faceless God*, and many others, including the Corpse Fauna cycle: *The Dead Bear Witness, Tears of Blood, The Dead in Their Masses*, and *The Eyes of the Dead.* He also writes the Machinations Sundry series of steampunk stories. He edited the Bram Stoker Award-nominated anthology, *Under Twin Suns: Alternate Histories of the Yellow Sign* and co-edited *A New York State of Fright* and *Even in the Grave*, an anthology of ghost stories. His website is: www.jameschambersonline.com.

A new voice in the genre of speculative steampunk, Ef Deal's short fiction has been published in numerous online zines and anthologies as well as in *F&SF*. Her short story *Czesko* was given an honorable mention in Gardner Dozois' *Year's Best Science Fiction and Fantasy*. A freelance editor for over thirty years and a member of SFWA and HWA, she is currently an assistant fiction editor at *Abyss&Apex* magazine and video editor for *Strong Women — Strange Worlds*. Her steampunk series from eSpec Books debuts with *Esprit de Corpse*, featuring the brilliant 19th-century sisters, the Twins of Bellesfées Jacqueline and Angélique. Hard science blends with the paranormal as they challenge the supernatural invasion of France in 1843. When she's not writing, Ef marches old-school alumni drum and bugle corps on soprano bugle; she also composes, arranges, and directs music. She lives in Haddonfield, NJ, with her husband Jack and her chow chow Corbin. Her website is www.efdeal.net. Follow her blog *Talespinner* at efdeal.blogspot.com.

Once Upon a Time, **Christine Norris** thought she wanted to be an archaeologist but hates sand and bugs, so instead, she became a writer. She is the author of several speculative fiction works for children and adults, including *The Library of Athena* series, *A Curse of Ash and Iron*, and contributions to *Gaslight and Grimm* and *Grimm Machinations*. She is kept busy on a daily basis by her day job as a school librarian in New Jersey. She may or may not have a secret library in her basement, and she absolutely believes in fairies.

David Lee Summers became a steampunk in 1987 when he used a nineteenth century telescope on Nantucket to examine the evolution of distant pulsating stars. Since that time, he has published thirteen novels and numerous short stories and poems spanning a wide range of the imagination. *Owl Dance, Lightning Wolves, The Brazen Shark,* and *Owl Riders* comprise the Clockwork Legion steampunk series. His other novels include *The Astronomer's Crypt, Vampires of the Scarlet Order* and *Firebrandt's Legacy*. His latest novella is a World War II-era cryptid tale called *Breaking the Code*.

David's short stories have appeared in such magazines and anthologies as *Realms of Fantasy, Cemetery Dance, Straight Outta Tombstone, Gaslight and Grimm,* and *After Punk*. He's been twice nominated for the Science Fiction Poetry Association's Rhysling Award.

In addition to writing, David has edited the science fiction anthologies: *A Kepler's Dozen, Kepler's Cowboys,* and *Maximum Velocity: The Best of the Full-Throttle Space Tales*. When not working with the written word, David operates telescopes at Kitt Peak National Observatory. Learn more about David at www.davidleesummers.com.

Beth Cato hails from Hanford, California, but currently writes and bakes cookies in a far distant realm. She's the Nebula Award-nominated author of *A Thousand Recipes for Revenge* from 47North (June 2023), plus the steampunk *Clockwork Dagger* duology and the *Blood of Earth* trilogy from Harper Voyager. Her short stories can be found in publications ranging from Beneath Ceaseless Skies to Uncanny Magazine. In 2019 and 2022, she won the Rhysling Award for short speculative poetry. Her website BethCato.com includes not only a vast bibliography, but a treasure trove of recipes for delectable goodies. Find her on Twitter as @BethCato and Instagram as @catocatsandcheese.

Hildy Silverman writes speculative fiction of all kinds, primarily for anthologies. Her story, "The Six Million Dollar Mermaid," was a finalist for the WSFA Small Press award. Her novella, *Invasive Species*, was released in 2023 as part of the Systema Paradoxa Cryptid Crate series published by eSpec Books. From 2005-2018, Hildy was the publisher and editorin-chief of Space and Time, a venerable magazine of fantasy, horror, and science fiction. She is a past president of the Garden State Speculative Fiction Writers and a frequent panelist on the science fiction convention circuit. For more information about Hildy, please visit www.crazy8press.com and www.hildysilverman.com.

About the Editors

Greg Schauer has been a bookseller for over 33 years as the owner of Between Books in Claymont Delaware. He has also helped produce concerts by local and national bands at the Arden Gild Hall in Arden Delaware, one of the countries oldest continuously run secular utopian art colonies, for the past 10 years. He has previously worked on Stories in Between: Between Books 30th anniversary Anthology with W.H. Horner and Jeanne Benzel and Steampowered Tales of Awesomeness Vol 1 by Brian Thomas and Ray Witte and With Great Power with John L. French. He can be contacted at gschauer@betweenbooks.com.

Award-winning author, editor, and publisher **Danielle Ackley-McPhail** has worked both sides of the publishing industry for longer than she cares to admit. In 2014 she joined forces with Mike McPhail and Greg Schauer to form eSpec Books (www.especbooks.com).

Her published works include eight novels, *Yesterday's Dreams, Tomorrow's Memories, Today's Promise, The Halfling's Court, The Redcaps' Queen, Daire's Devils, The Play of Light,* and *Baba Ali and the Clockwork Djinn,* written with Day Al-Mohamed. She is also the author of the solo collections *Eternal Wanderings, A Legacy of Stars, Consigned to the Sea, Flash in the Can, Transcendence, The Kindly Ones, Dawns a New Day, The Fox's Fire, Between Darkness and Light,* and the non-fiction writers' guides *The Literary Handyman, More Tips from the Handyman,* and *LH: Build-A-Book Workshop.* She is the senior editor of the *Bad-Ass Faeries* anthology series, *Gaslight & Grimm, Side of Good/Side of Evil, After Punk,* and *Footprints in the Stars.* Her short stories are included in numerous other anthologies and collections. She is a full member of the Science Fiction and Fantasy Writers Association.

In addition to her literary acclaim, she crafts and sells original costume horns under the moniker The Hornie Lady Custom Costume Horns, and homemade flavor-infused candied ginger under the brand of Ginger KICK! at literary conventions, on commission, and wholesale. Danielle lives in New Jersey with husband and fellow writer, Mike McPhail and four extremely spoiled cats.

Our Intrepid Adventurers

A.S. Etaski
Alexander H.
Alicia M Rabb
Allyn Gibson
Alp Beck
Amaia Belasko
Andrew Cook
Andrew Hatchell
Andrew Kaplan
Ann Stolinsky
Anonymous Reader
Anthony R. Cardno
Avatar-of-Chaos
Avis Crane
Aysha Rehm
Becky B
Beth (Peldyn) Sparks-Jacques
Bill Kohn
BOBBY ZAMARRON
Brad Goupil
Brad Jurn
Brad Kabosky
Brandy H
Brendan Lonehawk
Brendan Pease
Brian, Kay, and Joshua Williams

Bridget Engman
Brooks Moses
Caitlyn Price
Carol Gyzander
Carol Jones
Carol Mammano
Chad Bowden
Charlie Russel
Chris Newell
Christopher D. Abbott
Christopher J. Burke
Cindy Matera
Coleman Bland
Crohnicgamer
Crysella
Cullen Barr
Cynthia Radthorne
Dagmar Baumann
Dale A Russell
Danielle Ackley-McPhail
Danny Chamberlin
David Keener
David Lahner
David Myers
Denise and Raphael Sutton
Dianne Nicholson

Doc Coleman
Donna Hogg
Douglas Yeager
Dr. Nina B. L. Urban
Dusk Zer0
Ef Deal
Elaine Tindill-Rohr
Elizabeth Crefin
Ellery Rhodes
Eric P. Kurniawan
Eron Wyngarde
Frank Michaels
Fred Bauer
Fred Rexroad
Gail Z. Martin
Gary Phillips
Gav I
Gene Mederos
Gina DeSimone
GraceAnne DeCandido
Greg Levick
Hadrosaur Productions
Ian F Bell
Ian Harvey
J Piper Lee
Jace Chretin
Jacen Leonard
Jack Deal
Jacob H Joseph
Jakub Narębski
James Johnston
Jeanne M Hartley
Jeff Young
Jenn Whitworth
Jennifer L. Pierce
Jeremy Bottroff
Jessica Fortin
Jim Thornberry
John L. French
John Markley
John Ordover

Jon Quigley
Judy McClain
Julian White
June Chase
Karen Mitchell Carothers
Kate Cserjes
Kate Tabor
Kathryn Black
Kathy Brady
Keith R.A. DeCandido
Kelly Pierce
Kevin A Davis
krinsky
Lara Beneshan
Lara Struttman
Lauren O'Byrne
Lilia Millner
Lillian Taylor
Lisa Kruse
Liz DeJesus
Lori Beard
Lorraine J Anderson
Louise Lowenspets
Luis Leal
Lynn Pottenger
LZ
M. T. Hall
MAllder
Margaret Bumby
Marie Devey
Mark E Thompson
mark roth-whitworth
Mary Ann Shuman
Mary Jane Hetzlein
Maureen Hart
Megan Struttmann
Mel Follmer
Melissa Honig
Michael Axe
Michael Barbour
Michele Hall

Morgan Hazelwood
Mubarak Sadoon
Murky Master
Mustela
Nathan Turner
Nova Sisk
Otter Libris
pjk
PunkARTchick "Ruthenia"
Raphael Bressel
Regis M. Donovan
Richard Novak
Richard O'Shea
Richard Parker
Robby Thrasher
Robert C Flipse
Robin Lynn
Rusty Waldrup
Ruth Ann Orlansky
S. Evans
Saul Jaffe
Scantrontb
Scott Pearson
Scott Schaper
Shawnee M
Shelby Elenburg
Steph Parker

Stephanie Lucas
Stephen Ballentine
Stephen W. Buchanan
Steve & Beckey Sanchez
Steven Purcell
Susan J. Voss
Tawney Cooper
Therese Moore
Thomas M Karwacki
Thomas P. Tiernan
Tim DuBois
Tim Lonegan
Traci Belanger
Tracy "Rayhne' Fretwel
Tracy Popey
Trainor Houghton-Whyte
Trip Space-Parasite
Walter J. Montie
white beard geek
Whysper Wude
Will Gunderson
Will McDermott
william myers
Wingnut
Xanthe W.
Yosen Lin

Printed in the USA
CPSIA information can be obtained
at www.ICGtesting.com
CBHW020452020324
4767CB00001B/6